BIG BAD

By: Lynn Leite

By Lynn Leite

By Lynn Leite

1

"Wait a second, I'll go with you," Ellery called to Jasmine as she tried to sneak out the door.

For the last week, Jazz hadn't been able to go on her daily hike alone thanks to all of her other well-meaning housemates.

The week before she had slipped and fallen, dislocating her shoulder, which was still in a sling. Now, her housemates were determined that she shouldn't go on her daily walks alone. It would be another week before she could remove the sling and, hopefully, go back to her solo trips.

"You don't have to come, Ellery. I'm perfectly capable."

"I know you are, but we all worry. We didn't know where you were or what happened to you when you fell."

"I have my trusty cell phone and my new hiking boots that Alice got for me."

Jazz had been without a phone and wearing worn sneakers the day she slipped and fell onto her side. Her dislocated shoulder was useless in helping her climb back up the slope she had slipped down. She had been left with no choice but to wait until someone found her.

"Please humor us, at least until the sling is off."

"I don't mean to sound like I'm trying to get rid of you, El." She was trying to get rid of her but still appreciated the concern.

"You are trying to lose us or you wouldn't be sneaking out," the woman smiled as they left the old Victorian.

"I take walks to clear my mind and just be quiet. That's hard to do when another person is with you."

"I get it. I do I love just being silent. I do a lot of meditating. You are right. It's nearly impossible if someone is with me that doesn't get it. Alright, I'm sure you will be just fine but make sure you have your phone." Ellery had stopped following Jazz but still looked worried.

Jazz showed the woman that she did have her phone and took one step onto the path before feeling guilty. "Come on, Ellery. You are right. I should wait until the sling is off to go solo."

"Are you sure? I don't want to be in your way."

"I'm sure. I'd rather you come than Mary Grace."

"Oh, are you two not getting along?" Ellery asked, catching up to Jazz on the well-worn path.

"We get along fine. She just doesn't get the point of a quiet walk in the woods. She talks the entire way."

"She is a talker," Ellery laughed. "I will stay quiet. You won't even know I'm here."

"I like your company, don't get me wrong. I just want to go back to the silent walks I was enjoying."

"It's like your form of meditation."

"I guess so. I can't say I ever actually meditated."

"What is it that you normally do when you're alone?"

"I walk and think. Sometimes, I sit on a rock and just listen."

"That is meditation, Jazz."

"Whatever you say. You are the expert."

"I'm no expert," Ellery said softly, then they both fell into a comfortable silence.

Ellery looked like she would be right at home at Woodstock. Her flowing garments and wild strawberry blonde hair were a throwback to the 1960's. In addition, she was into crystals, Tarot cards, and the paranormal. She burned sage in the house once a week to cleanse it.

At first, Jazz found her strange, but in the last weeks, living in the same space, she was beginning to like the woman's carefree spirit.

Six women and the owner, Blythe, making it seven, lived in the old Victorian in the middle of nowhere. Jazz didn't know exactly where they were and neither did the five others brought there to a town that they called Blue Rock as part of the Witness Protection Program.

What or who they were being protected from was still unclear? Jazz was sure there was more to the story and Alice, the Therapist that came to see them practically daily, had confirmed that they didn't know the whole truth. That just made Jazz question everything.

"Left or right?" Ellery asked as they came to a fork in the path.

"You choose," Jazz smiled. The woman had been true to her word and walked silently beside her for the last half hour.

"Left," Ellery said with confidence and they resumed their stroll.

"Can I ask you something?"

"Of course," Ellery smiled.

"Do you ever ask your friend, the one that got in trouble and made you all a target..."

"Eve?"

"Yes, Eve, do you ever talk about what happened to her? It had to be bad if it made all of us targets by association."

"Yes, I have asked and yes, it is bad," Ellery said hesitantly.

"Can I ask what she says happened?"

"Look, Jazz, I know that the same thing happened to your brother and he didn't survive. Do you really need to know the details?"

"I think I do. I'm here in the middle of nowhere in a Witness Protection Program for something I didn't witness, living with strangers, no offense."

"None taken."

"I would say I lost everything, but that's only half true. They brought some of my things when they came to get me. I don't know how they got into my apartment to get them. That is just another mystery, but I am grateful. At least, I have some pictures and clothing."

"They got some of ours as well."

"I think that maybe knowing what happened, how my brother died, will make me believe more."

"What don't you believe? We all felt the headaches. I was in a coma by the time they got to me."

The women had been suffering from headaches that went beyond the norm. The searing pain would have eventually killed them. Jazz had no doubt that part of the story was true.

"I wasn't that bad yet, but I was in the hospital. I couldn't think straight, it hurt so bad."

"And now it doesn't. Truthfully, I don't care if I'm getting the whole story. I'm alive and I feel great. This place is beautiful. The people here are warm and welcoming."

"I just feel like I'm missing a piece."

"You are missing your brother."

"Yes, that's why I need to know what the others say happened."

"Eve said she was drugged. She woke up chained with others in a basement before being moved to a warehouse."

"Did she say why?"

"They were experimented on. She didn't go into detail and we didn't press her."

"What did she tell you about being rescued?"

"She told us that twelve people were chained in the space. When the Rescue team arrived, only nine were still alive."

"Maybe, she knew my brother? She might have seen him and spoken to him before he passed."

"I think you could ask her or Tate, Devlin, and Camryn. They were all with Eve, as well as others."

"I will ask. I think it might help. I still don't see how what they went through links to us."

"Easy, according to Eve, they picked people without a lot of relatives and close friends."

"Eve had the three of you."

"Yes, but to the outside world, we just looked like old roommates. People didn't know we went back to the third grade and were closer than most sisters."

"You are an odd group," Jazz said. "Sorry, that slipped out."

"We are an odd group, just like the six of us in the Safe house are an odd group, but it works."

"Yeah, you guys are growing on me," Jazz teased.

"So back to why us, from what Eve said, we were all drugged with something made to affect the memory. They didn't want anyone to go looking for the people they took. The twelve at the warehouse were not the only ones taken. Seven made it out alive before that. That's how they knew to go looking for the others."

"That is a lot of Missing people someone might have noticed."

"Right, so we didn't remember Eve, but our subconscious, or something like that, did remember her. The emptiness in our heads was what was causing the headaches."

"Empty heads, is that a Medical term?" Jazz rarely smiled, but it was hard not to when Ellery was around.

"No, of course not. I don't even begin to understand it. All I know is I was dying and now I am not. I'm sorry your brother didn't make it, but at least you are safe now."

"Safe from who or what?"

"Good question, I don't have the answer, but does that really matter? I trust Eve and I'm not on death's door, so being here for a while or forever is a win in my mind."

"You are an optimist. I'm a pessimist," Jazz pointed out.

"You have to admit that you're better off here than in the hospital."

"Yes."

"You could always go back home after they catch whoever did this."

Jazz thought for a moment whether that would be something she wanted. So far, the town of Blue Rock had more people in it that cared about Jazz than her hometown ever did.

"I think I'd still stay," Jazz said aloud.

"I'd like that. You're good company."

"Me, good company?" Jazz laughed.

"See, you're smiling and laughing. It's nice."

"Yes, it is," Jazz agreed. Perhaps, taking Ellery on her hike was a good choice.

2

Just as Jazz and Ellery turned back, Jazz got the strangest sense of being watched. She had felt this once before, just after she slipped and dislocated her arm. At one point, sitting on the shore of the nearby lake, she was sure she wasn't alone. Minutes later, the Mayor and Alice had come out of the woods calling her name.

"What is it?" Ellery asked, looking at Jazz.

"I feel like someone is out there. Hello," she called, scanning the surrounding woods. She saw nothing.

"We should get back," Ellery said, looking nervously down the path.

"I felt the same thing just before Alice found me. I think it was one of the guards watching."

"That would make sense. They are there to guard us," Ellery sounded relieved. "I don't see anyone or hear anything."

"I didn't either the day I fell. Then, like magic, this giant man came out of the shadows. I swear I thought it was Sasquatch."

"He was a guard."

"Yes, Alice and Blake introduced him. He gave me his shirt," Jazz said, recalling the man and his chivalrous act. He hadn't said anything, but his gesture meant a lot.

"A giant, hairy man came out of the shadows to give you his shirt," Ellery joked.

"He wasn't hairy. He was big and yes, he gave me his shirt. I haven't seen him since."

"But Alice knew him?" Ellery sounded nervous.

"Yes, his name was or is Vaughn and he is the one that found me. They told me that he waited until they got there because he didn't want to frighten me. You don't frighten me if it's you out there, Vaughn," Jazz called.

"Jazz, maybe it isn't Vaughn and it's a bear? is it wise to keep yelling like that?"

"If it's a bear, I should yell. You are supposed to make a lot of noise, I think. It's probably just my imagination, Ellery."

"You don't think something is out there now?"

"It was probably a squirrel watching from the trees." Jazz could see that Ellery was getting nervous. She still felt like someone was watching but not in a threatening way. There was no reason to make Ellery worry.

"As much as I'd like to see Sasquatch, I think I'll pass," Ellery smiled.

"I thought you loved the idea of witches, ghosts, and vampires, all that stuff?"

"I never said anything about vampires. Undead bloodsuckers actually existing is ridiculous. I know a few women that call themselves witches. I'm convinced that ghosts are real, so are a lot of other things, I bet."

"'There are more things on heaven and earth, Horatio, than are dreamt of in your philosophy'," Jazz recited.

"You're quoting Shakespeare?" Ellery laughed.

"It seemed appropriate. I did go to school, you know."

"I wasn't judging. I feel the same. There's more to this world than we might ever know."

"I'm alright with being blissfully ignorant. Life has kicked me in the gut too many times for me to go looking for trouble."

"If you ever need to talk, I'm here."

"Thank you, Ellery, and if you ever find the real Sasquatch, run."

"I will," she laughed, letting the silence take over once again as they walked back to the house.

Alice's car was parked in front of the house when Ellery and Jazz came out into the yard.

"There you are. We have company," Aya, one of Ellery's childhood friends, called from the porch.

"Did we miss group or something?" Jazz looked at Ellery for an answer.

"Not that I know of."

Alice and sometimes Eve's handsome husband, Kingston, held weekly Therapy Group sessions with the women. It helped to talk about the pain they experienced, the disorientation of being brought to the Safe house and the confusion as to why. Jazz had personally asked Alice what was really going on. The woman had assured her that she would, one day, have the whole story. That just confirmed that there was more going on here than met the eye but still didn't tell her what it was.

For now, she just had to trust the system. It wasn't easy for her to trust anyone, but she was working on it.

"Jazz, Ellery, this is Emerald. She's Blake's secretary and new to town like you are. I thought I'd introduce you all."

"Are you in the Witness Protection Program too?" Sarina asked.

"We aren't supposed to tell people we are in the Program, Sarina," Tasha rolled her eyes. "You keep blabbing and they will find us."

"Sorry, it slipped," Sarina apologized.

"Emerald is aware of your circumstance," Alice laughed, "but Tasha is correct that you should probably come up with another story."

"Like what?" Aya, the rational one in the group, asked.

"How about you are just making a new life here and leave it at that. People tend to fill in the blanks on their own," Alice suggested.

"A new life, that's what this is, so that's what I will tell people. How long have you lived here, Emerald?"

"I inherited a house from a long-lost Uncle. We have been here for a few months. I just started to work for the Al... the Mayor," Emerald smiled.

"You said we. Are you married?"

"No, I have a daughter, Gwen. She is three."

"Oh, I love kids. Is she here?" Mary Grace looked around as if she missed a three-year-old in the room.

"No, she convinced Nico to take her to the store."

"Tall, dark, and dangerous is taking a three-year-old to the store," Mary Grace sighed.

"Don't mind her. She has a crush on Nico and Eli and the other one. Was it Jett or Cole?" Tasha teased.

"They are all on my radar. There's no harm in looking, is there?" Mary Grace defended.

"No, and you are right. They are all eleven on a scale from one to ten. Just remember, looks aren't everything. Your ex was good looking and an asshole," Aya reminded.

"Keith was a looker with no soul," Mary Grace said sadly

"He's in jail now for the rest of his life," Alice added.

"Well, if Emerald let Nico take her daughter to the store, then he's probably not dangerous. Are you dating him?" Mary Grace asked Emerald.

"No, I think Nico has a bit of a harem when it comes to the local women. I'm not one of them. He is good with Gwen and she adores him."

"Nothing sexier than a man who loves kids." Mary Grace obviously had plans for Nico and Jazz couldn't say she blamed her. Like Aya said, they were all an eleven. The town had a lot of good-looking men.

A shadowy face of one man in particular came to mind. He wasn't handsome in the traditional sense. He was more rugged and manly. She still had Vaughn's shirt and planned to keep it. Maybe, it was hero worship or just the mystery of the quiet man that intrigued her. She was still wondering if he had been following her on her walk with Ellery as the women all sat sharing thoughts and ideas.

Emerald and Alice stayed for lunch before heading out. Jazz could see her becoming a friend. Normally, Jazz was not a fan of women. She found them petty and mean, but this group, as eclectic as it was, seemed to champion one another instead of putting each other down.

3

"We are meeting the Alpha female at three," Eli told Vaughn as he entered the Guard house.

"Senior Center?" Vaughn asked.

"No, the storefront, I think they are delivering the X-ray machine today. We are setting the place up to act as a makeshift clinic."

"I'll be there." Vaughn took off the backpack he had been wearing and opened the refrigerator to find something to eat.

"How did it go today?"

"Fine, Ellery went with her. I think Jazz is trying to dump the women, but they are persistent."

"You weren't seen?" Eli asked.

Vaughn knew that they were trying to give the women their freedom at the same time they were watching them. If one or more of them ran across a shifter mid-shift, they wanted to know about it to do damage control.

"I still don't know why the Alpha doesn't sit the women down and explain the real reason they are here and the truth about what we are," Cole added from across the room.

"Alice has helped the Shadow Pack seven and the nine others that the Moon Valley took in. They had been altered, so there was no easing them into our world. Six humans are a different thing altogether."

"I trust Alice," Jenkins added as the room filled, since it was lunchtime.

"See, Jenkins knows her better than all of us." Eli didn't normally use Jenkins as an example. The man was self-centered and obnoxious, but he was an excellent guard.

"Jazz was asking Ellery about the paranormal today on her walk."

"Like what?" Eli suddenly seemed a bit more serious.

"She mentioned ghosts, witches, and vampires," Vaughn offered as he stacked meat onto a roll.

"No mention of shifters?" Cole sounded insulted.

"No, they did say that Jazz thought I was Sasquatch at first."

"You are Sasquatch. I'm going to start calling you Sasquatch instead of Ghost," Jenkins taunted.

"I wouldn't recommend it," Vaughn glared at the man. He tolerated and even embraced the moniker of Ghost. He prided himself on being silent but deadly.

"I was kidding. Lighten up, Ghost."

"So, Jazz thought you were a Sasquatch for real," Eli smiled.

"She wasn't frightened, more surprised when I showed up the night she fell. The weirdest thing happened today. I think that Jazz knew I was there."

"You said they didn't see you."

"They didn't and Ellery said nothing, but Jazz mentioned feeling like she was being watched. She called out to me."

"She what?" Eli exclaimed.

"She yelled 'Vaughn, if that's you out there, you don't frighten me', something like that."

"She could just assume one of us is shadowing them in the forest. You came out of nowhere when she got hurt," Cole shrugged.

"I almost answered her," Vaughn looked to Eli. Now that Nico had moved up to the Alpha's Second position, Eli was in charge of the Guard.

"I suppose you could answer her. You can talk to Alice about what is best."

"If she knows you are there, then there is no sense in hiding. It might be better for her to know someone is actually there than feeling uncomfortable," Cole added.

"Are you losing your edge, Ghost? A human knew you were tracking her," Jenkins taunted.

"You are walking a fine line, Jenkins," Eli warned. "Ask Alice what she thinks would be best," Eli told Vaughn before asking the others how their day had gone so far.

Vaughn was grateful when the subject changed. He wasn't sure why or how Jazz knew he was there. It could have been a good guess on her part.

When Vaughn arrived at the storefront that was being transformed into an Urgent Care clinic, his Alpha, Blake was out front, directing a huge truck as it backed toward the doors.

"Ghost, thanks, go, we need all the muscle we can get," Blake smiled. Vaughn was only a couple of inches taller than the Alpha and slightly bulkier. He had physical strength that might match the Alpha's, but Blake exuded a power that only a true Alpha could possess. Vaughn, although he was Alpha Born, had no desire to be a pack's Alpha. He liked his place in the Pack and in the Guard.

"I'm at your disposal," Vaughn answered, looking at the huge crate in the back of the truck.

"We have an issue," Blake said softly.

"What issue?" Vaughn stepped in closer. The Alpha was keeping his voice down intentionally.

"Human driver and an 800-pound machine."

Vaughn nodded his understanding. Between the Alpha and himself, they could easily lift and lower, as well as carry in the machine. Shifters had the strength of two humans on average. Vaughn and Blake were not average.

"Eli has Cole and Jenkins joining us, I think." Vaughn scanned the main street for either man.

"Good, Alice is on her way. She can distract the driver," Blake smiled, seeing Alice and Emerald coming down the street.

The women went to work, speaking to the driver as the Alpha and Vaughn moved with quick precision to lower the machine to the ground and in the doorway to the vacant storefront.

"Thanks, Guys, we couldn't have done it without you," Blake waved down the street to no one.

His ruse worked and the driver stood with his mouth agape at the empty back of his truck. "How the hell…" he muttered to himself.

"We had help," Vaughn said, towering over the driver. The Human male did what most males did around Vaughn. He stepped back.

"Wow, okay, then are we good?" he asked Blake.

"Yes."

"Hold on," the man rushed to get a clipboard and handed it to Blake." Please sign here that it was delivered in one piece."

"Here you go," Blake signed and handed it back to the man, who was looking at Vaughn as he backed toward his truck and waved.

4

"I think you made him nervous," Alice laughed as the man drove away.

"Humans can sense a predator," Blake laughed, nudging Vaughn's arm.

"Speaking of which, Alice, can I have a word about one of the women staying with Blythe?"

"Is something wrong?" Alice asked, immediately assuming the worst.

"No, I just have a question."

"Go ahead."

"I am pretty sure that Jazz is aware I'm following her."

"She might assume she was being followed by the Guard since her accident," Alice agreed.

"I mean she knows it's me. This morning, she was walking with Ellery and said she felt like she was being watched. Then, she called out to me, saying 'Vaughn, I'm not sacred of you' or something to that affect."

"Interesting, what's the question that you wanted to ask?"

"Should I let her know I am there or stay in the shadows?"

"I don't know how you go unnoticed in the first place. I say, use your own judgment. If she calls out to see if you're there, it could be that she's frightened by the unknown. In that case, let her know you're there."

"And if she makes no more mention of it, then what? I know Eli has us tailing the women just in case they see something. She was talking to Ellery on the walk about her interest in the paranormal."

"Ellery already suspects something is different around here and Jazz is observant. If she calls to you or any of the guards, let her know you're there."

"I will. Thank you for your advice."

"Thank you for caring about their feelings."

"That's my job." Vaughn tipped his head, looking confused.

"No, Vaughn, your job is to guard them. Watch for a time they discover what's really happening. That doesn't require caring. You care."

"Yes, I do."

Blake stood with his mate as Vaughn left, waving off the others who had come too late to help.

"What was that about?"

"He just needed my advice. I do want to revise my guess on who at the B&B will discover our truth first."

"Oh, you don't think it will be Ellery."

"She's a good bet, but I am going with Jazz."

"The one with the shoulder?"

"Yes, I think that your Ghost might be letting the cat out of the bag sooner than later."

"I'm not following."

"I think that maybe Vaughn is interested in more than just guarding and shadowing the woman."

"You are matchmaking now? I thought that was Nico's specialty. Vaughn is good at his job. He takes every assignment seriously. Shadowing Jazz, who insists on wandering alone through the forest, is his assignment."

"We shall see," Allice smiled as she watched the man disappear into the Guard house. "I'm going to ask Blythe to keep an ear out."

"Are you sure the best course of action wouldn't be to just tell the women? They have been here for over a month. They trust us to a point," Blake questioned as he escorted Alice and Emerald back to the Pack house.

"I think that I trust the other Human women who didn't get a choice and were turned without permission. They think it is best to wait to let them figure it out in their own time," Alice shrugged.

"Can I add something?" Emerald asked as they headed back to the Pack house. She was human and knew about shifters because she had lived there for months.

"Yes, I'd like your opinion," Alice smiled. You were unaware we existed when you got here."

"I was told immediately in a letter that this was a Shifter town. I dismissed it as being an old man's weird way of telling me the town was full of shifty people."

"How did you find out?" Blake hadn't been the Alpha back when she first moved to the area. She had been there for a couple of months before the accident that ended with the Pack losing its Alpha pair.

"My property is near a well-worn path that shifters use. I saw a lot of wolves but hadn't made the connection. I was telling the Alpha female, who I just thought was a nice lady who came to welcome me at the time, that I might purchase a rifle because of the wolves."

"She told you then that they weren't just wolves?" Alice smiled.

"Yes, then she shifted. I thought she was insane taking her clothing off like that."

"Seeing is believing."

"Yes, it is. I think that eventually the women will see something."

"Would you want to be told or would you want to discover it on your own? The others we rescued seem to think easing them into it is the answer," Blake asked Emerald.

"I don't think it's that easy. This morning, I met six very different women. I think you're going to get six very different reactions to your secret. I would want to know. I'm glad the Alpha female did what she did, even though it terrified me."

"It didn't terrify you enough to leave," Alice pointed out.

"I had nowhere to go, so no, I didn't leave."

"Then, what would you suggest?"

"The hippy one, Ellery, she was talking about the legends and mysteries surrounding the house."

"Blythe gets most of her reservations that way. They think the woods are haunted and full of the paranormal," Blake nodded.

"Then lean into that, start with rumors of shifters as well as all of the other stuff. Make them curious and intrigued. The more I learned about real shifters, the more I saw you all as people who turned into wolves, not the slathering monsters that the media makes you out to be."

"I have never slathered on anyone," Nico called from the porch of the Pack house, where he sat watching Gwen draw on the sidewalk with chalk.

"I wasn't actually speaking to you," Emerald snapped, clearly annoyed by Nico inserting himself into the conversation.

"Thank you, Emerald, that is a great idea. I think you're right. The more realistic portrayals of what we are really like, the better. I think that Lila, the Shadow Pack's librarian, has some true history. We can plant the seed so that when they do discover the truth, they won't be frightened,"

"Oh, they will be frightened. You stripping and then morphing into a wolf is terrifying."

"I don't morph. I glide," Nico teased.

"Fine, you're free to glide now. Thank you for keeping an eye on her."

"It was a pleasure. Now, if you'll excuse me, I have a date."

"Same girl or is this someone knew?" Emerald asked.

"What business is it of yours?" Nico growled.

"It only becomes my business when they call incessantly to speak with you and you ask me to lie for you because you are out with someone else. Being your shield was not in my original job description."

"Then tell them I'm out."

"You're out alright, out of your mind. How about I start telling them the truth?"

"Go right ahead. I am a free man: no wife, no mate, no fiancé."

"You are absolutely right. I can't wait until your mate shows up and you have to explain the harem. I want a front row seat when you try to get rid of them."

"It's a Shifter thing. You wouldn't understand, but she will."

"Then, you'd better hope she isn't human."

"Let me know when you two are finished," Blake asked, clearly enjoying the banter.

"Sorry, Alpha," Emerald said softly.

"Nico, she's right. Six women thinking they are the only one spells disaster. Emerald, just tell them you're not Nico's secretary and hang up. He has a cell phone they can call."

"He doesn't give them his cell phone and the few he has given his number to say that he doesn't answer his cell. That's why they call the Pack house."

"I will answer my phone. I'm sorry I bothered you, Emerald," Nico seemed sincere.

"I forgive you. Thank you for taking care of Gwen."

"She's the only woman currently not giving me a hard time," Nico laughed.

"Maybe, you should listen to Emerald. Six women, Nico!" Alice scolded as Emerald gathered Gwen and her things to head out for the day.

"It's not like I am sleeping with all of them," Nico said, throwing up his hands.

"On that note, we are on our way. We will see you all tomorrow." Emerald waved before high-tailing it home.

5

"This is fascinating," Ellery said as the six women went through some of the books and handwritten accounts of Local legends.

"Werewolves, you can't be serious, Sarina groaned. "That's so overdone. I mean, come on."

"Vampires are overdone. Wolf shifters are sexy," Mary Grace added.

"You think every man you see is sexy, Mary Grace. Maybe, try to be more discerning. The last pretty face you dated almost killed you."

"I'm looking and not touching. They can't all be bad," she shrugged.

"Leave Mary Grace to her fantasy. There's nothing wrong with that. If she actually finds a real man to latch onto, we will make sure he's not a creeper," Aya announced.

"Amen to that, he will have to meet the approval of all of us, werewolves and vampires included," Tasha declared. They were joking with each other about Mary Grace and her terrible taste in men, but they were serious about protecting her.

Jazz just listened as they thumbed through the stack of Local legends that Alice had found to show Ellery. It was fascinating. It wasn't like Jazz believed in anything she couldn't see or feel, but it was entertaining.

"Look, they don't need the full moon to shift," Sarina pointed at a picture of a rather attractive man next to a picture of a wolf.

"That never made any sense to me," Ellery grinned.

"Have you thought about werewolves on the regular?" Tasha taunted.

"I think about all possibilities," Ellery countered. "These stories come from somewhere, not just here. Legends about ghosts and vampires, even werewolves, come from all over the world."

"Don't forget Sasquatch," Sarina chimed in.

"I think Jazz even believes in that one." Ellery looked at Jazz to see if she had gone too far.

"I'm a firm believer that something or someone was out there the other day," Jazz affirmed.

"Yet, she wanders the forest everyday alone," Tasha pointed out.

"I wish. I haven't been alone in two weeks. Alice, can I take this stupid sling off?"

"Yes, you can," Alice laughed as Jazz didn't hesitate to take the sling off before Alice finished.

"Now, maybe I can go back to hiking solo. No offence, Ladies, I appreciate you having my back, but I'd really like to take a walk alone, at least every once in a while."

"A brisk walk every day is healthy if you need the quiet alone time, as long as you bring your phone and take it easy, I don't see why not," Alice said, knowing her opinion mattered to the women.

"I think better alone and the forest sort of recharges me. I don't feel all that alone, if that makes sense."

"It does," Alice agreed. She also knew that, since Jazz fell, Vaughn had been ordered to shadow any of the women who went more than a few yards into the surrounding forest.

Alice was not sure that the others' response to Vaughn would be a good one. The man was intimidating and, despite Jazz having seen him before, she wasn't sure that even Jazz wouldn't be frightened if he just appeared.

After speaking to the man days before, she was sure that Jazz suspected he was following her on her walks. How she knew and why was another story. According to Blake and the other guards, the man they called Ghost was never seen.

Jazz sensing his presence and specifying that it was him could mean any number of things. Either Jazz wanted to believe the man was watching over her, or she truly had a Sixth sense that he was there. Time would tell.

"You heard her, Ladies. I get to walk alone if I want to."

"We just want you safe. You scared us. We all have lost so much."

"I thought you were running," Tasha said with a shrug.

"Running to where, I don't even know where we are, other than Northern New York."

"Exactly, I knew she wasn't running," Ellery insisted.

"If I decide in the future to run or leave, I promise to tell you I'm going."

"Good to know, that goes for all of us. If we go, we let the others know."

"Are you ladies thinking about leaving?" Alice asked, starting to be concerned in the direction the conversation had taken.

"Not me," Ellery smiled, "I'm staying, maybe forever. I hope eventually to get my own place. I feel sort of bad that Blythe has us here instead of paying renters." Ellery looked to the owner of the Victorian.

"Trust me, I'm well compensated for housing all of you here. Plus, I get to know all of you," Blythe assured her.

"I have nowhere to go," Mary Grace added.

All of them answered Alice, indicating that they were either afraid to leave or had no problem staying put. That might change when they found out they were in a Shifter town and not in the Witness Protection Program, but for now, it seemed they were content.

"Blythe, have you ever seen a werewolf in these woods.?" Ellery's question stunned Alice. They had decided not to lie outright if asked a direct question. The question Ellery asked couldn't be more direct.

"How would she be able to tell? Look at the description here. They look regular then poof." Sarina held up one of the books Alice had brought.

"Poof, is that a technical term?" Tasha laughed.

"I'm serious. If they look like any other person or a regular wolf, then how can you be sure they don't exist?" Ellery sighed.

"In that case, I might have seen a few werewolves and not known it," Blythe skillfully answered with a true statement.

Alice sighed her relief. She didn't want to lie to the women. She just wanted to have them slowly discover the truth.

"She's right. How would we tell unless they turned into a wolf right in front of us?"

"Ellery, people are going to look at you funny if you start asking if they have seen werewolves," Aya warned

"I asked Blythe and she has people here all the time looking for some Paranormal creature or another, right?"

"I do have a lot of Ghost hunters and Paranormal investigators. Something about this house being on a ley line. I don't know what that means. The house was my Gran's, then my Dad's before he passed it to me."

"Was it always a B&B?"

"No, that was my way of keeping the place. It helped that word got out of strange sightings."

"You mean someone saw a German Shepard and thought werewolf?" Aya shook her head.

"Not exactly," Blythe laughed.

Blythe was good at deflecting the women from the truth. She was part shifter. Her father was a shifter. Her mother chose to remain human. Blythe was born mostly human and didn't have the ability to shift, but she grew up surrounded by shifters and their families.

6

"I have my cell phone, two bottles of water, three protein bars, and I'm wearing hiking boots, bug spray, and a windbreaker. The guard outside, Eli, said they can track our phones if needed," Jazz told Aya, who was still not a fan of Jazz hiking alone.

"I'm sorry, just be careful." Aya knew she was being over the top.

"Don't be sorry. It's nice to have someone looking out for me."

"I want to believe we are safe here and that if someone is looking for us, they can't find this place."

"I'm not even sure they are looking for us, but if they are, I don't think they are wandering the forest hoping to find one of us alone," Jazz said sarcastically.

"You have a point there."

"I was hiking alone for weeks before I fell. The most dangerous thing I encountered was a squirrel."

"Did you grow up near a forest?" Aya asked, walking with Jazz to the edge of the yard.

"I grew up in a suburb. We had woods nearby that we played in but nothing like this."

"It is something. Alice said most of the land here is State Park. It goes on for hundreds of miles."

"I don't plan on going hundreds of miles today, maybe a mile or two. I'll call if I'm going to be late for dinner."

Jazz waved to Aya and started down one of the paths that led from the yard. She didn't say a word and kept walking for a few hundred feet before turning to look behind her. She half expected Aya to be there with her.

She took her time, breathing the fresh air tinged with the scent of what Blythe called petrichor. It had rained the day before and the warm rain combined with the dry land gave off an earthy scent.

She had walked for nearly an hour, heading toward the old quarry that Alice had shown her. The sound of a small waterfall hit her heightened senses. The flow of water from the top of the quarry barley reached waterfall status. It was more of a dripping, but after yesterday's rain, it was a bit more than she had recalled.

Finding a nice spot to just sit, Jazz looked through the break in the trees. A sort of man-made lake left over when the quarry closed was sparkling in the mid-day sun.

The feeling of being watched washed over her again. Jazz stood, doing a three sixty scan and seeing nothing.

"Hello?" Jazz called.

Any one of the women could have followed or one of the guards. Jazz's stomach tightened at the thought of one particular guard. She still had Vaughn's tee-shirt shoved under the pillow she slept on. She knew it was a weird thing to keep. The fact that the man had given her his shirt to make a sling was still fresh in her mind.

She felt his presence out there. Either that or she was going crazy.

"Alright, whoever is out there, can you please just let me know? Vaughn, is that you?"

"Yes," a low masculine voice came from behind her, causing her to spin around to see where the voice came from.

Vaughn stood there as if he had materialized out of thin air.

"I didn't mean to frighten you."

"I wasn't frightened. Do you always follow us?"

"Only since you fell," Vaughn seemed amused. "How did you know I was there?"

"I'm not sure. I sort of felt eyes watching me."

"How did you know it was me?" The man's brisk tone made Jazz think the answer might be important.

"You will think I'm crazy."

"I doubt it. I make it a point not to be seen or heard when I'm tracking. In my line of work, it could mean the difference between life and death."

"That sounds serious."

"It is very serious, Jazz."

"You know my name?"

"I know all of your names. We learned them when we were briefed on your situation."

"Of course, I forgot for a second that I even have a *situation*. It seems so normal here, except for the security, I guess."

"Are you going to tell me how you knew I was there?"

"I could smell you." Jazz turned red and looked at the forest floor.

"You picked up my scent, but you are hu… untrained."

Jazz could have sworn he was about to say that she was human. She was human and she was untrained, but Vaughn was human too, maybe superhuman from the look of him, but he was definitely all man.

"I have to stop hanging out with Ellery," she muttered to herself.

"What?" Vaughn looked right through her.

"You asked how I knew it was you and I told you. I smelled the same scent that is on your shirt. I mean was on the shirt you gave me the night I fell."

Vaughn made a strange noise that sounded almost like a growl. Jazz was starting to think she had fallen asleep and this was a dream. The god-like specimen of a man, who stood a full head taller than her, had appeared out of nowhere. She should be terrified, alone in the woods with a virtual stranger who just admitted to stalking her. She wasn't afraid. She was the opposite.

"You kept the shirt," Vaughn stepped closer and Jazz didn't budge, "why?"

"You ask a lot of questions," Jazz looked up at his face.

"The answers might be important."

"Because no one has ever noticed you following them?"

"They call me Ghost for a reason."

Jazz took a completely involuntary breath in as the man closed in. His scent surrounded her.

"Ghost," Jazz sighed.

"Yes, Jazz."

"Why is it that I want you to kiss me right now?"

"I was asking myself the same thing. May I touch you?" It was a strange request. Jazz couldn't recall a man ever asking permission to touch her.

"Yes."

7

Jazz couldn't remember ever being kissed the way Vaughn kissed her. In addition to her body responding immediately and her heart pounding, she felt a rightness about this. She felt wanted. She felt precious. For a big man, Vaughn knew how to handle a smaller woman.

As the kiss slowed and the man holding her pulled back to look at her, Jazz started to giggle.

"I'm not sure if I should be offended by that reaction." He didn't look all that worried.

"I just realized I'm in the middle of the forest with a man they call 'Ghost', making out like I'm sixteen in the back of my Dad's Chevy, and I'm hoping the moment never ends."

"All moments end, but there can be more moments."

"Please tell me you're not married or in a relationship? I'm not asking for anything like a commitment or even more than just this, Ghost. I just don't want to be doing something that would hurt someone."

"No wife, no girlfriend, not in a while. I will warn you that I do have an ex who is annoying at times."

"How long has this ex been an ex? Wait, I'm sorry. It's none of my business."

"Maybe, I want to make it your business. She has been an ex since September."

"Wow, and she's still hopeful?"

"I couldn't say what's in her head. Now that I have met you, she doesn't stand a chance."

"Do you say that to all the girls?" Jazz was surprisingly comfortable chatting with this imposing man as he held her.

"No, I can assure you I am breaking all sorts of rules right now for you." His words were full of promises.

"That's right. You are on duty."

"That is not the rules I am referring to but yes, I am on duty, technically."

"No one has to know you kissed me or that I even saw you. We are both adults. It's not wrong. It doesn't feel wrong."

"Jazz, you and I being together is complicated, but it isn't wrong."

"You want us to be together. Ghost, I don't normally do this."

"Don't do what, meet men in the woods?" he smirked

"You are not just any man. I can't explain it."

"You don't have to. I feel like we were meant to find each other."

"Vaughn… Ghost, whoever… I hope you are not just telling me what you think I want to hear."

"I have no clue what you want to hear. I'm telling you what I feel."

"That proves it. I'm just dreaming," Jazz exclaimed, stepping back a bit before she started pacing as Vaughn watched. He wasn't going to push her. She needed to come to the conclusion that he was meant for her in her own time. It was a good thing he was patient.

"You believe that you are asleep?"

"You tell me. I obsess over a man because he does one kind thing. I sleep with his damn shirt under my pillow. Then, you appear out of nowhere and kiss the hell out of me. Now, you're saying all the right things, telling me that we are meant for each other."

"Do you disagree?"

"No, that doesn't mean I understand it."

Jazz's cell phone's shrill ring startled her.

"You had better answer that," Vaughan smiled. Jazz blinked, expecting him to disappear, but there he was, looking like a fallen angel, sitting on the rock she had stopped to rest on.

"Damn, is it really six?"

"About that," Ghost smiled. "We were distracted."

"You can say that again. What do I tell them?"

"Jazz, you can tell them the truth. Just let them know you are alright."

"Right, okay… Hello," Jazz stared at Vaughn when she heard Blythe on the other line.

"*Just checking in, where are you? Aya and Ellery are ready to come after you,*" Blythe chuckled.

"I'm still down by the quarry."

"Tell her I'm here with you." Ghost stood and engulfed her in a hug.

"*Was that Ghost?*" Blythe sounded surprised.

"Yes, Blythe, I have her," Ghost answered Blythe before Jazz could decide what to say. She's fine. She just lost track of time. She will be on her way home soon."

"*Alright, is there anything I need to know?*"

Jazz found the question a strange one. What would Blythe need to know? Maybe, she thought Jazz had gotten hurt again.

"Nothing you need to know yet," he said, disconnecting and handing Jazz her phone.

The look Vaughn gave her held so many promises it sent her mind reeling. Was she now sort of seeing the man they called "Ghost", like dating, or was it just a hook-up, even if they hadn't hooked up? Given enough time, Jazz was sure that was where they would have ended up.

"I guess I should get back."

"I'll walk with you, if you don't mind?" Ghost fell into step with Jazz as she walked slowly down the path to the house.

"Do you prefer Ghost or Vaughn?"

"Either, most people call me Ghost."

"Ghost it is. So, what now? We should get the awkward discussion over with before I read far too much into what just happened. You go first."

"You want me to decide where we go from here?" he asked, giving her an incredulous look.

"Yes, men tend to steer the relationship, even if the woman thinks that they are. Not that I'm pushing for a relationship, I just don't know where we are going, or if we are going anywhere?"

"You are cute when you're confused."

"No one ever called me cute, Ghost. I'm dark, broody, mysterious, and maudlin, but not cute."

"That is a matter of opinion. I will lay this out for you, at great risk."

"Risk?"

"Risk of you turning tail and running. I want to see you again. I want to kiss you again. I want much more than that, when the time is right. I see this as the start of a very long-term relationship. I know you are just adjusting to living here, so it's your call."

"I have a question and how you answer it makes a difference in my answer."

"Alright."

"I know for a fact that there is more going on here than just six women in a Witness Protection Program. I still haven't figured out how my brother dying ended up targeting me. Alice assured me I would be told the whole truth eventually."

"That isn't a question, Jazz."

"No, my question to you is do you know the reason I'm really here?"

"Yes."

"If I asked, would you tell me the truth?"

"If you asked, I would tell you the truth."

"Alright, I'm not even sure I really want or need to know."

"You don't need to know right now but soon."

8

Jazz looked back as she broke through the tree line. Ghost stood there watching to make sure she got inside safely.

She had decided, as they approached the house, that for now, Ghost was going to be her little secret. Until she was sure this was what she hoped it was, there was no sense in telling the women in the house. Aya would, no doubt, worry that Jazz had been making out with a man she just met while alone in the forest. Mary Grace would try and find her own guard to sneak off with.

This was fast and intense. Jazz had never felt this kind of instant connection to anyone before, so she didn't trust it.

"There she is. I was worried."

"I was fine, Aya. Blythe called. She told you I was fine."

"Yes, but you could have been held hostage and your captors made you say you were fine."

"You maybe need to talk to Alice and Kingston about your spiraling dark thoughts, Aya. No one is out there. No one will find us. Have you seen the guards? Even if they did find us, we would be safe."

"I know. You are right. I just hate waiting for something to go wrong. This place is a dream. The people here are so nice. I'm waiting for the punch line."

"Maybe, there is no punch line. Maybe, what you see here is what you get."

"At the risk of sounding like Ellery, there is an air of mystery here."

"I feel it too. I don't see the unknown as always being a bad thing," Jazz said softly.

"I didn't think you were an optimist." Aya tilted her head to the side and smiled.

"Things are looking up. My arm is healed. The weather is getting warmer. I'm making friends."

"I'm glad to see it. You seemed so sad all the time when we got here."

"I am saddened by my brother's passing. I'm saddened that I didn't know to honor him. I'm really sad about the way he died."

"You know how he died?"

"Not exactly, but if he was locked away and experimented on, like your friend Eve said, then it wasn't a peaceful passing."

"No, I'm sure it wasn't. Think of it this way. For him, it might have been a relief."

Jazz looked at Aya, wondering how the woman was always able to find some light in the darkest situations yet always worried that something was wrong."

"You have a point."

"Dinner is ready. Did you want to change first>" Aya looked down at the mud on Jazz's boots.

"I suppose I should. Tell the others I'll be right down." Jazz slipped the boots off by the door and went to put something else on.

Jazz was just putting on a pair of slip-on shoes when she noticed Blythe standing in the doorway.

"I came to see if you were really alright."

"I told you I was fine."

"Yes, but Ghost is called Ghost because he can be practically standing right next to you and you don't see him. If he was with you, I thought something might have happened for him to come out of the shadows."

"He came out of the shadows because I asked him to. I knew I was being followed and thought it might be him."

"You did?"

"Yes, I was right. He said he has been following us on our hikes since I slipped."

"I already knew that. I just didn't know you did. So, you said what to him?"

"I said, I know you're there, Vaughn."

"You knew it was him specifically?" Blythe came in and sat beside Jazz on the bed.

"You're acting like that's a big deal," Jazz said, wondering about the woman's reaction.

"It might be a big deal. Were you frightened?"

"Of Ghost, no, not at all. He literally gave me the shirt off his back and Alice vouched for him."

"Did he walk you back or did he disappear again?"

"Blythe, if you have some interest in Ghost…"

"No, oh no, nothing like that. It's just he is as his name implies, a ghost, yet you somehow knew he was there. He also looks scary as hell. Just his size is intimidating. Your reaction and your ability to sense he was there is curious."

Jazz debated internally whether to tell Blythe that she liked the man, maybe even more than liked him. She decided to go with her first instinct, to keep whatever was happening between them to herself, at least until she was sure what it actually was.

"I felt like someone was there and assumed it was him. I didn't see him until he wanted me to."

"Alright, I just wanted to make sure you were alright and not frightened."

"I'm not frightened of Ghost."

"Good, because I could always ask Blake to assign someone else to shadow your walks."

"NO!" Jazz said a little too forcefully. "If I have to have a guard shadow me, it has to be him. Someone I don't know would scare me."

"I get it. I don't think Ghost would want anyone else shadowing you either," Blythe smiled and winked. "Dinner is on the table. Let's go down."

"Alright." Jazz was confused by the direction the conversation had gone. She was also starving.

"Jazz, you know that you can ask me anything and tell me anything in confidence. All of you girls can. I want you to know that."

"Thank you, same goes for you. Are you trying to ask me something, but you're purposely not asking?"

"I suppose I am. It's none of my business, really."

"I think that maybe I'm not ready to answer the question you are not asking."

"Got it," Blythe grinned as they left the room.

"That has to be the strangest non-conversation I have ever had," Jazz laughed.

"Yes, yet it said so much," Blythe laughed with her.

9

Vaughn stepped through the front door of the Pack house, not expecting the small, Human female.

"You're big," the blonde cherub face toddler said as soon as he entered.

"And you are tiny," he said as another Human woman came out from behind the desk.

"Gwen, that's not polite. Can I help you?"

"I'm here to see Alice or Blake, preferably both." Ghost had spent the night trying to figure out how to ease Jazz into the idea of a permanent relationship.

"Who should I tell them is here?"

"Ghost or Vaughn, I go by either."

"Have a seat. Gwen, I need you to tell Miss Alice we have company. Can you do that?"

"I can do that," the three-year-old grinned before running out of the room.

"She is adorable." Ghost could hear the flutter of fear coming from the chest of the human as her heart sped up.

"She's precocious. I'm Emerald. Are you one of the Alpha's guards?" Ghost knew she asked one question for two reasons. If Ghost was one of the guards, that would make him safe. She also had called Blake the Alpha intentionally, showing she knew that he was a shifter.

"Yes, is it that obvious?"

"Like Gwen said, you are big."

"Ghost, everything alright?" Alice came out of the kitchen holding the tiny cherub's hand.

"I need to speak with you and probably Blake as well."

"He's in his office." Alice motioned for him to follow, nodding at Emerald. Her heart rate had slowed back to nearly normal now that Alice was there.

"Blake, we have company." Alice swung the door open and motioned for Ghost to go in first.

"To what do I owe the pleasure?" Blake asked as Ghost folded himself into one of the chairs in front of the Alpha's desk.

"I need advice or permission."

"Which is it?" Blake clasped his fingers together on the desk.

"One of the women at Blythe's is my mate," he said point blank. There was no sense in sugarcoating it.

"You are sure?" Alice asked

"Absolutely," Ghost turned to the Alpha's mate.

"Let me guess. Jasmine, am I right?" Alice smiled.

"Yes."

"Does she know?" Blake asked cautiously.

"Yes and no."

"Explain," Blake barked.

"I was shadowing her. I have every time she went out since the accident. She knew I was there, Sir. I don't know how she knew, but she knew."

"You're sure of that?"

"Yes, she called to me said she knew I was there, so I showed myself. Sir, she said she could smell my scent in the air."

"That is unusual for a human," Blake looked to Alice.

"It is unusual but not all that unlikely she had your scent. This at least explains her desire to keep your torn shirt," Alice smiled.

"What was her response when you came out of the shadows?"

"She was not frightened. She seemed glad to see me, then she asked me to kiss her."

"Just like that?" Blake looked surprised.

"No, there was more to it. I kissed her. Sir, she is mine. Her response was undeniable. I believe that she feels the same. I made sure to tell her I intended to make our relationship long term. She didn't believe me."

"In the Human world, both men and women will lie to get what they want. What else was said?"

"Nothing that would indicate I was not human, if that's what you are asking."

"It is exactly what I was asking. Alice, if Jazz is his mate, she has to know what he is before she can commit or reject him." Blake looked to his mate for an idea of how to proceed.

"She's not rejecting me," Ghost growled.

"No one suggested she would Vaughn," Alice soothed. "She's human, she is in a strange place. She's lost her brother and, most importantly, she doesn't know what you are. How can she make any informed decision when one of the most important facts are hidden from her?"

"I agree she needs to know the whole truth," Blake nodded. "The question is how and when?"

"I think we could ask someone to weigh in on this that might know better than the three of us." Alice stood and opened the office door. "Emerald, could you come in here for a second?"

The woman appeared in the doorway with Gwen on her hip. "Is there something you need?"

"Yes, we need advice."

"From me?" Emerald scanned the three faces in the room, looking for the punch line.

"Yes, you, please have a seat?" Blake gestured to the couch on the far side of the room. "I take it you have met Ghost."

"Ghosts are scary," Gwen chimed in.

"I'm not that kind of ghost," Vaughn smiled at the three-year-old. He knew he was large and imposing. No one ever messed with him and didn't regret it afterward. He didn't want this little girl to fear him.

"Gwen, Ghost is just a nickname, like I call you Gwennie sometimes and Nico calls you Princess. You're not a real princess, are you?"

"No," Gwen wagged her head side to side then up and down in understanding.

"What do you need help with?" Emerald settled Gwen on her lap and handed her a toy as she listened.

"Ghost is one of our guards. He has been tracking the women at the Safehouse to make sure they don't get lost or hurt."

"Like Jazz and her shoulder," Emerald acknowledged.

"Exactly, Jazz is healed enough to go off on her own now and something happened today."

"Was she hurt?" Emerald looked concerned.

"No, she knew I was there," Ghost said to the Human woman that had been manning the desk when he got there. "I am called Ghost because I am never seen. Shifters and humans alike don't know I'm there until I want them to."

"Yet, Jazz knew you were there."

"Yes, she knew I was there. She sensed my presence once before and I thought it might just be her guessing. It wasn't. This afternoon, she called to me by name."

"I'm not sure what I can add to help you. Some humans are sensitive, I guess. Some claim to tell the future. I'd say I don't believe that's possible, but after moving here, I'm going with everything is possible," Emerald shrugged.

"Your introduction to our kind is why we called you in here. What do you know about Shifter matings?" Blake asked to get the ball rolling.

10

"Alright, let me see if I have this straight. You found Jazz when she got hurt. You gave her your shirt as a sling."

"Yes."

"Then, you followed her every day to make sure she is safe. I'm not saying you're a stalker," Emerald smiled weakly.

The man sitting by Blake was intimidating. He looked like a gladiator or a warrior. There was nothing soft about him. His personality and voice were what had put her at ease.

"I was assigned to follow but remain unseen."

"I'm not sure how someone your size remains unseen. You said she smelled you?"

"She's human. Even shifters can't find me, even when they know I'm there. She knew I was out there, me specifically, and when I asked, she said she had smelled me, that the air smelled like my shirt. Can humans do that?"

"Apparently, Jazz can. We have a pretty good sense of smell, not as good as yours."

"Emerald, Ghost showed himself to Jazz and they had an encounter." Blake looked at Gwen, who had fallen asleep, bored by the inactivity.

"Oh, an encounter?" Emerald gasped.

"Not what you are thinking. What Blake means is he touched her," Alice explained.

"I am starting to follow. That's why you asked if I knew about Shifter mating."

"She is my mate," Ghost told the Human woman. "She responded to me as if she felt the same."

"I've heard of love at first sight, even between us humans. It's pretty rare, but it happens. You are sure?"

"Absolutely sure."

"And you called me in here for advice? I'm a single mother whose baby's daddy ran for the hills before the test even came back positive."

Alice smiled at Emerald, trying not to laugh at the woman's comment. "We need your advice on how to introduce the fact that the town is full of shifters to Jazz. She needs to know before Ghost can discuss a future."

"I'd say that would be a big deal. Are you worried she will run screaming?"

"Yes," Ghost affirmed.

"And we want just her to know, not all of them at once?"

"I think the timeline for easing them in just moved up, but for Jazz, it's now imperative for her to make an informed decision about Ghost."

"Yes, '*Surprise, I'm a shifter*' on the honeymoon would be a bad start to any marriage."

"What should I do?" Ghost pleaded.

"I found out because the Alpha B-word stripped down and shifted in front of me. She was sort of ripping the band-aid off, so to speak. I was told there were shifters here, but I didn't believe it. These women haven't been told."

"I brought them books about the area and the legends of shifters and other things existing, like you suggested."

"Fairy tales are one thing. Reality is a bit different. It might get them thinking about shifters, but they still won't actually believe they exist. A live person shifting in front of you is the only real proof and, even then, I was wondering if I had imagined it. If this Human woman is feeling what you called the Mating pull, she needs to know about all of this. I can't imagine if Gwen suddenly started to shift and I had no clue shifters were real."

"It won't come to that. If Ghost and she are intimate, then it's rare for a human or even a shifter to get pregnant without the Mating bond," Alice told Emerald.

"Good to know. That's convenient. Not a lot of human men around here and, eventually, I might want to get back to dating."

"It's not full proof, Emerald."

"Oh, I was talking about the Mating instinct. It is good to know a human can feel it. I wasn't talking about... you know."

"Emerald, do you have any advice on how to proceed with Jazz?"

"Yes, but you are not going to like it," she said to Ghost.

"Why won't I like it?"

"I think you should take it slow. I met Jazz only once. She was quiet and sort of sad. I know her brother died and that explained her mood. If it was me in her position I don't know if 'Hey, I'm your mate and, by the way, I can turn into a wolf' is the way to go right away. She doesn't trust the explanation of why she's even here. No matter how much she feels about you after one encounter, I think a little wooing would be in order. Show her you care, make plans, show up for them. Show her that she can trust you."

"Are you sure that's wise?" Alice asked.

"Why wouldn't it be?" Emerald shifted Gwen to the other arm as she spoke.

"If she trusts him completely, then he drops the bomb that he's a shifter. Wouldn't that undo most of the trust?"

"You have a point," Emerald said softly. "I already knew about shifters and the way I was shown worked. You could just shift in front of her, but I recommend telling her first. Even if she thinks you're insane, the actual shifting will go better if she has some idea."

"So, basically, there's no good way to do this," Ghost sounded defeated.

"If she's yours, she will come around even if she runs," Emerald said with confidence. "We aren't all that different. We want the truth. We want trust and we want love and caring. You already care and, from what you said, she trusts you. Maybe, start by telling her there is more to you than meets the eye. Give her hints. Let her know you and get to know her. I don't think there is any right answer here. I would want to know up front what I was dealing with. I say tell her, show her, but ease her into it."

"Thank you, Emerald, you have been a great help. Do you need help getting Gwen in the car?" Blake stood, extending his arms to take the child.

"Thank you, Alpha."

"We will see you tomorrow, Emerald," Alice called as Blake carried the child out and Emerald followed.

"I'm sorry if that didn't help at all."

"It actually did help. I need to gain her trust before showing her. It's just hard."

"You want to go get her right now and take her home."

"That would be a problem. At the moment, I live in the Guard house. I'm not bringing a mate there."

"And you living with the women is a huge no. I think, tomorrow, we need to get you a house."

"There are some old shacks down on the other side of the quarry. There was a tornado that took most of them out and no one bothered to rebuild. I could claim one of them and, with a little work, it could be nice. Jazz likes the forest and the quarry."

"That is a wonderful idea," Blake was back and had heard the whole thing.

"There are several small homes unused there. Eventually, these women will all need homes of their own. You have my permission to choose one that's to your liking. I will talk to May about supplies and we can get a crew out there to fix them all, even rebuild those that went down."

"Thank you, Sir. Can I show Jazz the area? I need to make sure she would like it."

"Ghost, you are going to be fine. You're already thinking like a mate. You have our blessing. I would prefer that Jazz keep your secret once she knows the truth, but it isn't a requirement. My advice is going with your instinct, let her know you are different sooner rather than later. Jazz won't be able to resist you," Alice gushed.

"I hope you are right."

11

Ghost was still unsure about what to do. The conversation with the Human woman and the Alpha couple had been all over the place. The one thing he was sure of was he had their blessing. He had an idea of where to make a home and he had permission to tell Jazz everything.

"Leaving the Pack house, he headed down the front walk, lost in his own thoughts.

"Oh, Ghost, I didn't know you'd be here," a shrill voice he knew all too well pulled him from his thoughts.

"Hello, Gianna." Ghost tried to step around the woman on the narrow path and she countered the move with practiced skill.

"Aren't you going to ask why I'm here?" She tried to sound seductive but all Ghost heard was whining.

"No, because I don't care why you are here."

"I'm going to go to The Den with Nico."

The Den, a local Shifter bar slash restaurant was a popular spot for first dates. She was trying to make him jealous and, instead, she was giving him hope that she'll finally leave him alone.

They were over nearly a year ago and he had avoided most women since then. Gianna took that as him pining for her and wishing he could have her back, since he didn't move on. The truth was he hadn't moved on for fear of another woman trying to cling to a dead relationship. One sort of stalker was enough.

"Good for you, bad for Nico," he snapped.

"It's new between us. I hope you understand?" The woman needed Drama lessons. She was a terrible actress.

"Mind, I'm thrilled! Does Nico know that this date is a relationship in your head? I thought he dated a lot of women."

"Unlike you, he's just making sure he has the right woman. Are you still waiting for me, Ghost? I'm right here."

"No, I can safely say I am not waiting for you. I found my mate and you are not her."

Ghost cursed under his breath. He shouldn't have said anything. Telling Gianna that he found his mate was to hopefully get rid of her. The problem was the look on her face. She was pissed. Her expression went from anger to disbelief and back faster than Ghost could keep track.

"Who?" she said between clenched teeth.

"I'm certain that isn't your business. We are not friends. We were a mistake and you have a date with the Alpha second."

"Is it Diane?"

"Who is Diane?"

"Diane over at the corner store, she flirted with you at the Christmas party last year."

"Gianna, I was not at the Christmas party last year. I was on duty. If you mean a year and a half ago, just before you cheated and we broke up, I don't recall any Diane."

"I cheated because you weren't paying any attention to me."

"Because we were on the way out and you didn't get the hint. You are not my mate. You were a terrible girlfriend and if you thought sleeping with someone else was going to change that, then you are delusional."

"I thought you'd be at least a little more upset."

"You know what, so did I. When I found you had hooked up with Jared, all I felt was relief. I saw you for the manipulative bitch you are. You wanted me to go kill Jared and tell you that you were mine. You weren't mine and all it did was prove that even dating you was a waste of my time."

"I don't have to stand here and listen to this. Where is this mate of yours? Shouldn't she be by your side? Unless, you are making her up."

"That's it. I'm making her up and you are in my way. Goodbye, Gianna."

"I knew you were making her up just to make me feel upset."

"Not everything is about you. Have a nice life, Gianna. I hope I never see you again."

Ghost smiled to himself, having noticed Nico was in the doorway listening. He liked the Alpha second. They had been friends for years. He wanted to warn Nico of the ramifications of starting up with Gianna, but the man was on his own.

As soon as he walked in the door to the Guard house, Eli signaled to him. "You and I need to have a word," Eli said, gesturing to the Lead guard's office, which Eli now occupied, since Nico had moved to the Alpha second position.

"Did Blake call you?" Ghost asked as the door shut behind them.

"No, is there a problem?"

"I just assumed he had called you. What did you need to see me about?"

"Jazz," Eli barked, then he waited for Ghost to react."

"I'm going to need more, Eli. What about Jazz?"

"Your scent was all over her when she returned from her walk. Blythe was concerned as well."

"Concerned that I molested her or took advantage?" Ghost was not happy if that was what they thought of him.

"No, neither of us thought you'd harm her, at least not physically. She's human, Ghost, and in a vulnerable position now. Why would you approach her? Why would she be covered in your scent?"

"I was just speaking to the Alpha pair about that."

"You were?" Eli knew that Ghost wouldn't lie.

"Jazz knew I was there. She called out. That is why I showed myself this time."

"That still doesn't explain why I could tell you have been together."

"She's my mate. I already informed the Alpha pair and got advice on what to do next. I would never hurt her or any of them. The fact that she's human is a bit of an obstacle, but I intend on claiming her soon, I hope."

"That was not what I expected. You think she was aware of you because, on some level, she feels it too?"

"She feels it. She doesn't trust it or know what it is, but she definitely feels it."

12

Jazz bolted out the door early that morning to go for her hike. She wanted to get an early start and avoid one of the others volunteering. She had almost made a clean getaway when Blythe called from the porch.

"Jazz, take this with you." Blythe held up a pack that was larger than the small bag she had tossed over her shoulder carrying water and protein bars.

"What is this?"

"Lunch for two, I assume you're meeting Ghost."

"I am not sure of that. I mean what happened yesterday could have been mostly me imagining something that wasn't there."

"The look on your face tells me there is a lot there. Go, I'm sure you'll bump into him before lunch. Call if you aren't going to make dinner."

"You're not worried about me out there alone?" Jazz smiled.

"You won't be alone. If he doesn't show, call me. I'll come have lunch with you and you can cry on my shoulder."

"I don't want to cry, Blythe. Maybe, I should just stay home for today." Jazz had worried all night that Ghost wouldn't be there when she walked. He could have spent the last day and night regretting getting involved. He might even be in trouble for crossing a line. He had said he was breaking rules.

"Go, he will be there. I just know it," Blythe assured her.

"You know a lot of things. Don't you, Blythe?"

"Yes, I do and if you need someone to talk to, come to me or Alice first."

"You think I will need counseling."

"I think you will be just fine."

"I hope so. I will call and let you know about dinner, or lunch if he doesn't show."

"Sounds like a plan," Blythe waved as Jazz took her first few steps into the woods.

Trying to stay calm was pointless. She was anxious, nervous, and hoped for the hundredth time she was reading the situation correctly.

She listened to every sound, yet still didn't sense he was there. She was a good fifteen minutes into her walk when she saw him standing in the path.

The urge to run to him overrode her Common Sense brain and she rushed to him. He opened his arms as she got there and relief flooded her. She held onto him, standing still in the middle of nowhere, just listening to his heart with her ear pressed against his chest.

"That was some greeting," Ghost said, stroking her hair as he held her.

"I wasn't sure you would be here and I wasn't sure that what you said yesterday was even real."

"I've been told it's Human nature to question, especially feelings that are this intense."

"They are intense, aren't they?"

"I'd say so. Did you sleep well?"

"Not at all. "

"I should have given you my cell number so you could call me, or I could call you."

"I wouldn't have called," Jazz admitted, pulling away slightly so she could see his face. "I would have wanted to and maybe even dialed once or twice."

"You didn't think I was being genuine about my feelings?"

"No men don't say stuff like that, not on a first date. Not that it was a date," Jazz started to get flustered.

"Stop thinking of what might be wrong. Nothing is wrong. I meant every word and I thought we might spend the day together, maybe get to know one another."

"Don't you have to work?"

"My job is to make sure you ladies don't get lost or hurt again."

"So, this is you working," Jazz grinned.

"This is me trying to convince a girl to give a guy a chance. I have something to show you."

"Oh, what is it?"

"You will see. Do you trust me?"

"Yes, Ghost, I trust you."

"It's this way," Ghost took her hand and they started toward the quarry.

The rock cliffs and pristine water below was always a sight that had a calming effect on Jazz. Ghost holding her hand was even more soothing.

They walked in a comfortable silence, Ghost slowing his pace to match hers through the winding path. As they walked around the lake to an area Jazz hadn't explored, she was marveling in the beauty of the surroundings.

"There is an actual road that comes around the ridge there, but I wanted your opinion," Ghost broke the silence.

"My opinion on what?"

"Right now, I live in a house with other Security people. I was thinking I'd take one of the homes here and fix it up to live."

"Homes?" All Jazz saw was forest.

"Just to your left." Ghost pointed through the trees and Jazz could see there were structures.

"Your eyes must be better than mine. I can barely make that out."

"My people have great eyesight," Ghost said, intentionally hinting he was different.

"Are you native to the area?"

"Yes, several generations now."

"It has to be nice knowing your history. My brother and I were both adopted. I don't know where I came from."

"Family doesn't have to be biological."

"My brother was my Bio-brother. We had the same parents. He was a year older. I was one when our parents took us in. They were an older couple who hadn't ever had children. Our father used to joke that we were our Mom's mid-life crisis. They were good, loving people. I was grateful to have them."

"They are gone?"

"Fate is a bitch. A car accident took our real parents and cancer took both of our adopted parents. They died a year apart. My mother could not live without my Dad. I think she would have survived the cancer, but she lost the will to fight. I always said she died of a broken heart."

"Is that why you are unwilling to believe I'm sincere?"

"That's why the idea of you being sincere scares me. I both long for that kind of connection and fear it."

"I can imagine not wanting to live after losing a Life partner. I have seen many older couples follow one another into the next life."

"I like the way that sounds when you say it."

"Death is the only real guarantee in life. A long life filled with love, ending together is something I do not fear."

"Do you have a secret notebook of all the right things to say?"

"No, I am just speaking from the heart."

"I would have guessed you to be more… I don't know, lethal."

"I can assure you this is only my response to you. I am considered lethal. I know people fear me and I use that to my advantage. I am a guard. I protect the town, its people, and visitors from any number of things."

"Like ghosts, vampires, werewolves, and witches, that is what's rumored to be in these woods. Am I right?"

"Don't forget Sasquatch?" Ghost smiled, seeing another opening to ease her into the truth. "I can honestly say I have never actually seen any spirits or vampires here in Blue Rock."

"And witches?" Jazz smiled up at him as they walked.

"That might depend on your definition of a witch. We have a coven nearby and Blythe has had more than one either genuine or self-proclaimed witch stay at the B&B."

"I had a seventh-grade teacher we called a witch."

"Exactly, I would say I've seen my share."

"And werewolves?"

"The politically correct term is Wolf shifter," Ghost said with caution.

"Yes, of course, let's not offend the wolves. Oh, this is what you were pointing at," Jazz exclaimed as they broke through the trees. Ghost was grateful for the change of subject. He had told her the truth. They did prefer Wolf shifter to the Werewolf moniker. He hadn't denied seeing them. He was easing her into this, but he knew lying would be a disaster.

"A tornado came through about ten years ago. The electrical and internet lines were just repaired recently. The whole area looked like a war zone. Some of the houses are still in good condition."

"Doesn't someone own them?"

"The town bought the residents out, so they could start fresh in a new home."

"Like I'm starting fresh here?"

"Sort of, I asked the Alph... Blake about making one of these my home. I can't live in the Guard house forever."

Jazz could swear that Ghost was about to call Blake Alpha. It was probably him messing with her, since she actually asked if he had seen a werewolf.

"And he just said, 'Sure, pick one'?"

"Yes, actually, he did. Will you help me pick?"

"Not that one," she laughed, pointing to one that had one side missing and half the roof off. The forest had worked hard to reclaim it in the last ten years.

"You aren't into early Apocalypse type housing?"

"I like a roof over my head."

"Then, let's find one with a roof," Ghost grinned.

13

Jazz stood looking out of a grime filled picture window at the other side of the lake and the sheer quarry walls made of granite just beyond.

The small grouping of homes was mostly intact. She could see that a few repairs had been attempted here and there. Ghost had said that the main reason for the houses being left unoccupied was the power lines being down and most of the road being decimated. A bridge out had caused many people to take the buyout offer of moving to another area.

"What do you think?" Ghosts' arms wrapped around her from behind. It was something couples did. He held her and she leaned her head back against his chest.

"What do I think about the view or the house?"

"About this place?"

"It's magical," she said without hesitation. "It needs work, but it's so beautiful. I would hate to leave if I had lived here."

"Without electricity and roads, it was hard for the people that lived here. They were mostly older."

"It's so secluded. I guess if I was elderly, this might be too wild." Jazz turned to face him, still in the circle of his arms. "The main question is do you like it?"

"If you like it, I do."

"Seriously, it's going to be your house, not mine."

"What if I told you I want you to live here with me."

"I would tell you that you are full of shit," Jazz blushed.

"You think that's a line from some notebook as well?"

"No, I think you actually mean it right now, in this moment." Jazz saw the seriousness in his expression. "You hardly know me."

"I know all I need to know." Ghost had been fighting the urge to kiss her, to do so much more, but the look on her face when she said he didn't know her was so hopeful, he lost the battle. He bent, kissing her slowly at first. Her arms shot up, wrapping around his neck.

"Watch your shoulder," he growled, fearing her sudden movement might have caused her more harm.

"I'm fine. Shut up and kiss me," she laughed, wrapping her legs around his waist as he lifted her to his mouth.

""Your eyes," Jazz said, not sounding at all fearful but more curious.

"What about them?" Ghost asked, closing his eyes and kissing down Jazz's neck to distract her. He knew what she had seen. His wolf was on the surface, pushing for Vaughn to claim the women he was holding.

"They changed color, more golden, oh yes, right there," she groaned as Ghost slid his hands up inside her shirt.

"Only for you. Jazz, if we don't stop now, I'm not going to be able to stop."

"I don't recall asking you to stop."

"You have to be sure."

"I'm sure I want you right now. I'm sure we can figure out the rest."

"Jazz, if I make love to you right now, there may be no going back. I am asking for forever here."

"I know better than to say yes to forever this soon. Can't we just be together?"

"We can," Vaughn said, taking the cover off of the couch the last residents had left and laying Jazz beneath him.

The Alpha was going to kill him and he would probably deserve it. He wasn't going to go as far as biting Jazz, or officially claiming her in that way, but making love to your mate, even if she wasn't yours yet, was a huge risk. She still didn't know he was a shifter. She still didn't know she was his true mate. She didn't know how serious this was, that he intended to spend a lifetime loving her.

"You are mine," he growled as he slowly undid her clothing. She hadn't taken her eyes off of him.

"I actually believe you mean that," she said as she fumbled, trying to get his shirt over his head.

"I do and I will prove it every day from now on."

"I look forward to that," Jazz said, wondering if the man was huge all over and if this next part was going to be a problem.

It was not a problem. It was perfect. She hadn't been with anyone in a very long time, but there was no denying this was different. The lethal giant claiming that she was his was gentle and loving.

So many emotions were churning in her head she nearly cried. She felt like his. She wanted to be his. The idea that this man could destroy her if he walked away now was terrifying. No one should be that invested in another person, especially this soon.

"Jazz," Ghost groaned as she met him, stroke for stroke, kiss for kiss, sensation for sensation.

Just as he thought his mind would burst, he exploded and his body followed. The couch broke, sending both of them rolling onto the floor.

Ghost's concern for Jazz had him instinctively curling around her to protect her.

Jazz laughing from beneath him was a huge relief.

"I think you might have to invest in stronger furniture," she giggled.

"Or a decent bed." Vaughn stood, helping Jazz up as he went.

This would be the perfect time to tell her the truth about the town. It was the perfect time to just shift and prove what she would surely think was a lie. He couldn't bring himself to possibly ruin this moment. No matter what she decided or how she reacted, he would have this moment.

"Wow you look even better naked than you do with clothing on," Jazz blurted.

"I could say the same for you. I love either look on you."

"I didn't really mean to say that out loud. What I meant is I'm not the kind of girl that is into muscles or naked guys in some girl's version of adult entertainment. I never really cared if a guy had a six pack or… you know what, I'm sorry I even started this."

"I understand. You don't judge people on their appearance."

"Right, sounds good, do you have any idea where my pants went?" Jazz blushed.

"No, I'm sure they are somewhere, but we don't need them right now," Ghost said, kissing her again.

"

14

"I don't want to leave," Jazz said, looking at the shoreline of the lake.

"We could stay here for the night," Ghost said as they walked the path around the lake. The houses overlooked the quarry and the lake that had been made generations ago.

"As much as I'd like to say yes to that, I think I need to go back. Aya would lead the search party, carrying torches if I wasn't home by dark. They don't know about you. They don't know I'm safer here than anywhere."

"You didn't mention me?"

"I did, sort of, to Ellery. Blythe already knew since she packed a lunch that could feed an army."

"I remember you said you knew I was there when Ellery was with you," Ghost laughed.

"I was right!" she exclaimed. "You were there. I knew it. Why didn't you come out of hiding? How the hell do you hide in the first place?"

"How I hide is a trade secret. The reason why I hid was because I didn't want to frighten Ellery. I wasn't sure it was a good idea to let you all know we are following you to keep you safe. I had to speak to Eli."

"Your superior."

"He is my boss, then next up the ladder is Nico and Blake, of course."

"Because Blake is the…. Mayor?" Jazz said slowly.

"In a manner of speaking, yes."

"I feel like I'm missing something, that all of us are missing something."

"Like what?" Ghost asked.

Instead of denying that they were missing something, Ghost had basically acknowledged that there was something without telling her what it was. They were alone and had just come together in the most intimate way. He had struggled not to bite her. She needed to know the truth, but Alice had suggested letting her ask the questions.

"Ellery believes the legends and stories we heard about this place are rooted in truth."

"What do you believe?"

"I'm starting to think she might be partially right. Every time I ask about how I got here and why we are being protected, I hear the truth, but I feel like it's only part of it. Alice, Blake, Nico, and all of you are leaving something out. Even Blythe is holding back."

"Was that a question?" Ghost smiled.

"Yes, you are holding back, right? There is more to this."

"Yes, there is more. We have told you all the truth but left out key information. No one has lied to you, Jazz."

"I need to know, Ghost."

"Yes, you do. Ask the question." Ghost wanted her to be his, but until she knew the whole truth, she couldn't be. If he had even the slightest clue how to tell her without her running, especially since they had been together, he would have told her already.

"Are you allowed to tell me what's going on?"

"I spoke to Blake about it. I am allowed to tell you because we are together. I can ease you into the truth, tell you outright, or let you figure it out on your own."

"Sounds mysterious."

"Jazz, the town has secrets. I can just tell you if you'd like. The sooner you know, the sooner we can just be together."

"Ghost, I hope to hell you're not feeding me a line."

"No line, I understand why you are questioning me, but I want to be with you. I want you to live here with me in one of these homes. The moment you know the truth, how you react will determine the rest of my life."

"I'm used to guys avoiding commitment. You are serious though, aren't you? You would move me in right now, wouldn't you?"

"I might give it a day or two to get some decent furniture and clean the place."

"Keep the couch," Jazz smiled, "it has sentimental value. We can just fix the broken leg," Jazz giggled.

"Is that the house you want?"

Ghost turned back to see the few houses still standing. It would be a lot of work to either rebuild or clear the others, but Blake said he thought the women would need homes eventually. Jazz would have her friends nearby. It was all going to work out. It had to.

Not telling Jazz the whole truth was starting to feel like a lie. Alice thought easing the humans into the fact that shifters existed was best. Ghost agreed, but this was his mate. He couldn't take her as a mate until she understood that mating was forever. She was human. There would be things she needed to consider. Did she want to turn or would she want to remain human? She would have to know that their children would likely be shifters, even if she was human.

"Ghost, where did you go just now?"

"What?"

"You were staring into space."

"I was imagining our life here."

"I'm starting to believe you," Jazz said softly.

"I need you to want the same thing, Jazz. It takes two to have a successful relationship."

"I want you. I want this. I want all of the promises you seem to be making. I just think it's too good to be real. I just slept with a man I've known for a week and, now, we are picking out houses."

"The Alph… Mayor said that fixing up these places would give all of you a place eventually. We wouldn't be alone here in time." Ghost had misspoken intentionally this time. He was seconds away from stripping and shifting to show her. The only thing holding him back was his fear of her rejecting him.

"I am inclined to just say yes, but I know I should think about it"

"Of course, I'm off tomorrow and I think I might go get that bed," Ghost smiled.

"Then, maybe get some paint. The color in the Living room is puke green."

"What color paint?" Ghost smiled. She was already on board. She just needed time.

"White, but not too bright, maybe eggshell."

"Anything else?"

"We will need everything eventually."

"Bed and paint for now. I'll pick up a few things to make it livable."

"Will I see you tomorrow?" Jazz asked as they headed back to the house she was staying at. The path was well worn, but the trip seemed shorter.

"Yes, I will call you when I get back. Give me your cell." Vaughn took the phone and put his nickname, Ghost, and his number, then programed himself to be #1 on Speed dial.

"Number 1, huh?"

"Yes, Jazz, and don't forget it."

"I wasn't disagreeing," she smiled, leaning into him as they raced the darkness. It was getting late and getting dark quickly. "Can you see the path?" she asked.

"Yes, I can see perfectly well in the dark," he said, guiding her toward the distant lights of the Bed and Breakfast. He was dropping all sorts of hints, hoping she picked them up.

15

"Look who decided to come back," Aya stood on the porch watching as Jazz and Ghost emerged from the tree line.

"Oh, I see how it is," Tasha taunted.

"I take it back. Tall, dark, and dangerous has been dethroned. That man is gigantic," Mary Grace gasped.

"This is Vaughn. Vaughn, that's Aya. Next to her is Tasha. You've seen Ellery before."

"He has?"

"I told you I thought we were being followed," Jazz reminded.

"You brought home your stalker." The expression on Sarina's face told Jazz that she was joking.

"He was not stalking. That's Sarina and the one with her mouth hanging open is Mary Grace."

"Ladies," Ghost nodded.

"Ghost is a guard, like Cole and Eli. He has been making sure we are safe on our walks."

"Ghost? "Ellery smiled.

"It's because I usually go unseen. Jazz is the first person to sense I was there in a very long time."

"Well, you can guard me anytime." Mary Grace was practically purring.

"Mary Grace, what did we say about that? That's the second man you thought was dangerous then hit on."

"I like to live on the edge," Mary Grace shrugged.

"The edge almost killed you," Aya scolded.

"He's mine, Mary Grace." Jazz glanced at the man beside her to see his reaction.

"Oh, so that's why you were late."

"I was showing her some homes we are renovating. When they decide you are safe, some of you might wish a home of your own."

"Oh, is that *all* you were doing?"

"Mary Grace, get your mind out of the gutter," Ellery snapped.

"On that note, I will be going. Jazz, I'll call you when I get back tomorrow."

"Sounds good, remember egg shell."

"Got it. Bye, Ladies," he waved, giving Jazz a quick kiss on the lips before walking off.

"Bye, Ghost." Ellery grabbed Jazz's arm, dragging her inside, then she faced Jazz. "He is yours as in you and he…"

"He and I are dating. It might be more speed dating at this point. He wants me to move in with him."

"You're giving him paint orders. Are you seriously considering moving out with a man you hardly know? Jazz are you out of your mind?"

"Maybe, I am. I was with him yesterday too."

"He is the one with the shirt, the one you have under your pillow."

"How did you know I had a shirt under my pillow?"

"You mentioned that you kept the shirt. The part about the pillow was just a good guess."

"I can't explain it, Ellery. It's like I have known him forever. Everything is just so easy with him."

"I will admit that you seem happier these last few days. Your aura is brighter. You said he showed you a house."

Jazz wasn't sure what an aura was, but she did feel brighter. "It's an area that has several houses. Most of them were damaged in a tornado a while back. The residents were elderly, so the town bought them out and re-housed them. It's beautiful."

"I can see it in your face. You are considering moving in with him. I can tell."

"He already spoke to the Mayor about it. It's just..."

"Just what?"

"He mentioned the town had secrets. He said there was more I needed to know. It was like he wanted to tell me, but I needed to ask the right questions."

"So, ask the right questions," Ellery bounced on her toes with excitement.

"How am I supposed to know what the right questions are?"

"Good question, I'll help you figure it out. I love a good mystery."

"I get the feeling that whatever the town's secrets are, they are huge."

"What are you two whispering about?" Blythe asked as came into the room.

"Ellery is grilling me about Ghost. He walked me to the door."

"Oh yes, he is a conversation piece. How was your hike?"

"Wonderful thank you for lunch."

"Anytime, if you need to talk, you know where to find me," Blythe waved as she crossed the room and went out the door.

"That was interesting," Ellery whispered.

"That Blythe knew about Ghost? She already knew I was meeting up with him."

"No, the part about if you need to *talk*," Ellery said, glancing at the door Blythe had just left through.

"You are enjoying this, aren't you?"

"Yes, I am."

16

"Are you walking today?" Ellery asked at breakfast.

"I'm not sure. Ghost was going into town to buy a few things. You heard him say he would call when he got back."

"You can't walk without your new boyfriend. That's how it all starts, you know. He tells you to wait for his call, then you can't go out even to the store." Mary Grace was clearly lost in her own thoughts.

"Mary Grace, he isn't your ex," Tasha barked at the same time Aya pointed out that she had flirted with Ghost the night before.

"Sorry, I just got carried away," Mary Grace looked down at the floor instead of at the ladies.

"I do not need his permission to go on my walk. I just thought I might wait for him."

"I was asking because I enjoyed our walk the other day and if you wanted company. I heard him say he would call when he got back.

"I can go for two walks today instead of just one. Does anyone else want to join us?"

"God, no, the humidity today is disgusting," Tasha whined, touching her hair.

"I am seeing Alice this morning," Mary Grace said shaking her head.

Aya and Sarina ended up declining as well.

"It looks like just you and me," Ellery smiled. "I'll get my boots." After Jazz slipped and dislocated her arm, all of the women were provided with brand new hiking boots so they would be more sure-footed in the forest.

"I let Blythe know we were leaving."

"Does that mean someone else will be following us?" Elery asked Blythe.

"No, I think Ghost was mainly following Jazz here," Blythe answered, handing both of them a lightweight pack to carry. "You have cell phones. The pack has a few essentials, including food and water. Call if you need help. I'll make sure Eli knows you went for a hike."

"Thank you," Ellery said as they started down the main path.

"Tasha was right. It is humid." Jazz stripped off the sweatshirt she had been wearing and tied it to her waist.

"Official summer is days away," Ellery added.

"True, I bet this place gets a lot of snow in the winter. Every house we looked at yesterday had a huge fireplace and a generator. Most were ripped off of the houses. It was weird seeing the abandoned town. Some houses were untouched. Others were kindling.

"Where is this abandoned village?"

"You make it sound haunted," Jazz laughed.

"It could be."

"I felt comfortable there, at peace."

"Because you have a man who clearly adores you."

"You think so?"

"I do. I might be against you moving in with a man you just met, but the way he looked at you said the feelings were real."

"I can't explain it really."

"You don't have to. For the first few weeks we were here, you were so sad and quiet. I really worried about you."

"And now?"

"You seem lighter. Happiness looks good on you. I hope this Ghost person is genuine."

"He is." Jazz was sure of it.

"How far away are these houses. I'm just starting to understand you and think of you as a friend and you're talking about moving out."

"How about I show you?" Jazz pointed toward the quarry.

"Lead the way." Elery fell in step beside her, taking the next right toward the quarry.

"Speaking of snow, how are you going to get home in the winters if you live out here?"

"Ghost said there was a road that came into the area from the other direction. I'm sure they have snow plows here."

"It was a stupid question. Of course, the people that used to live there had to have a way to get home."

"I'm sure this area has all sorts of nooks and crannies that we haven't even been to yet. We have never been into town, not that I think it's probably a huge town, but I'd like to know where I need to go to shop and stuff."

"Not until it's safe," Ellery said sarcastically as she rolled her eyes.

"You don't believe we are in danger?"

"No, not real danger, at least not here. I can't deny that I was on death's door before they came and Eve is the reason any of us are alive, from what I hear. No one thought to check on the friends and family of those taken before that."

"I'm glad they did. I'd probably be gone by now as well. Whatever drug they gave us to forget our loved ones was killing some of us. I heard some recovered and didn't require rescuing."

"Yes, Alice said as much. I guess the five of us were the stubborn ones."

"Five?"

"Yes, remember Mary Grace didn't know Camryn at all. It was her abusive boyfriend that was drugged. The only reason he wasn't hurt by Camryn's absence was that Mary Grace and Cam are identical."

"I only got part of that story. Alice took me for a walk every time you had visitors. She didn't want me to feel left out or remind me that my brother was gone."

"She means well. It has to be hard counseling all of us. We are all so different."

"That and whatever secret she's keeping."

"Ghost told you the town had secrets."

"Sounds like a made for TV movie, doesn't it?"

"Yes, I've been thinking a lot about it lately."

"So, have I. I asked Ghost about it."

"You did?"

"Yes, he said that he had honestly never seen a spirt or vampire in Blue Rock."

"Interesting that he used the word *honestly* like he wanted to assure you he was telling the truth. Did he say anything else?" Ellery was riveted.

"Yes, he said that there was a coven of witches nearby and that many self-proclaimed witches frequented Blythe's place."

"I heard the same. Did you mention the werewolves in the books that Alice showed us about Local legends?"

"Yes, I did. He said that the correct term was Wolf shifter, not Werewolf."

"Seriously?"

"Yes."

"Did he say he ever saw one or that it was just a story?"

"He didn't say anything else. I joked that I'd try and be more politically correct in the future."

"Hum?"

"What's hum? You don't actually think there are Wolf shifters in the woods, do you?"

"He said the witches were real."

"He said there was a coven. He didn't say they were real witches. It could be a group of Goth or Emo girls that share a house and call themselves witches to keep people away."

"It could be, but look at all the hints we have. Alice brings books with mainly shifters and witches as the content of local lore. Ghost talks about secrets you need to ask questions about and Blythe offers her time for you to 'Talk'."

"Are you saying I should ask Ghost if the town has Wolf shifters in it?" Jazz laughed as they came to the turn that led to the homes.

"Why not?"

"Because he likes me. I don't want him to think I'm insane."

"Is it insane really? We don't know half of what's really out there, Jazz. Aliens, other dimensions, fairies, *Wolf shifters,* witches, ghosts, there is so much we don't know."

"You are right. We don't know and some of us don't want to know. We are here. This is the village. Tell me what you think."

"About the house or about what is going on in this town?"

"The house for now."

17

The two women spent the whole morning wandering in and out of several of the homes. Jazz made sure they stayed out of the few that Ghost had deemed unsafe.

When they got to the one Jazz had picked, they entered through the back French door.

The dust covered floor and furniture was interrupted by a sure sign they had been there the day before. Foot prints and the three-legged couch with the cover tossed aside made Jazz smile.

"I'm not going to ask," Ellery laughed, clearly putting two and two together.

"This is going to be our house."

"God, I hope you know what you are doing. If this Ghost person lets you down, I'm going to have to kill him."

"You couldn't kill a fly the other day, much less a man like Ghost. I know how risky this is, but I can't imagine not trying."

"It is a beautiful spot. Maybe, I'll have to move in next door to keep an eye on you two."

"You are starting to sound like my mother used to when my brother and I would sneak out."

"I've been accused of being overly maternal, but most people don't notice since Aya is so much worse," Ellery shrugged, making Jazz laugh.

"Let me show you the lake. There's a beach and everything."

"You should have been a realtor," Ellery smiled as Jazz opened the doors.

The walk to the lake took only seconds and Jazz felt at home. The diamonds on the water where the late morning sun hit it was mesmerizing. Jazz imagined a bench there so she could sit and enjoy without getting sand in her pants.

"I'm sold, where do I sign up?" Elery sighed, leaning back with her face to the sun.

"Ghost said he talked to the Mayor…" Jazz stopped short, recalling that when Ghost referred to the Mayor, he either said Blake or he called him Alph, then switched to Mayor. If she told Ellery that, the woman would be full on Wolf shifter hunting.

"Annnd?" Ellery was staring at her.

"Oh, sorry, he talked to Blake about renovating these houses and them possibly being homes for all of us when it was safe."

"It's safe for you because you will be living with a one-man army. He reminds me of a gladiator."

"He's lethal for sure, but I trust him."

"Obviously, if you're shopping for homes. We should probably get back soon."

"I know. The others will worry." Jazz stood and brushed the sand off while Ellery did the same. She watched the woman shake her whole body to get the sand off her and out of her hair.

Anyone looking at the two of them would see polar opposites. Ellery was curly haired, strawberry blonde, dressed in flowing light clothing. Jazz had jeans, a black tee. Her dark brown, almost black hair was stick straight and knotted at the back of her neck. She was dark to Ellery's light.

"Which way?" Ellery asked as they got to a junction. Jazz heard something nearby, holding her hand up to Ellery while looking around.

"You do know the way back, don't you?" Ellery whispered.

"Yes, I just thought I heard something."

"If you are saying that to freak me out, you have succeeded," Ellery said, looking right then left.

"It could be nothing."

"Or it could be something."

"Ghost, if that's you, can you please come out? Eli, Cole, Jenkins, I don't know all of your names," Jazz yelled.

"Why are you yelling?"

"It's not like we can outrun a bear. Yelling might scare it away. We have already been through that."

"This time, you think it's a bear?" Ellery squeaked.

"For all I know, it was a fat squirrel." Jazz was trying to sooth Ellery's nerves while at the same time hoping that one of the guards appeared.

"A fat squirrel, be serious."

It was probably nothing. Let's just keep walking, Ellery. I don't think we are in danger."

"Think again," Ellery stopped short and Jazz nearly knocked her over.

"Don't move," Jazz said, looking past Ellery to the large, gray wolf standing on the path.

"I wasn't planning on it," Ellery hissed.

"It's probably as afraid of us as we are of it," Jazz said in a soft, soothing tone. Dogs responded to tone more than words. She hoped that was true for wolves.

"It doesn't look afraid, Jazz." Ellery stood like a statue as the animal approached, sniffing the air. "It wants the food in our packs," she decided and the wolf looked up at her with a strange expression, as if had understood her.

"I have an idea," Jazz said, taking a small step back to retrieve her cell phone. She was calling whoever had called her last." Keep talking to it."

"And say what, nice doggie?" Ellery hissed. "It could be a Wolf shifter. Calling a Wolf shifter, a doggie, might piss it off." Of course, Ellery would jump to that conclusion.

Jazz was about to admonish her for even suggesting it was a Wolf shifter when the wolf stepped back, cocked its head, then turned into a woman.

"Oh shit, I was right," Ellery was squealing.

The naked woman looked a lot less menacing than the wolf had, but only slightly.

"Jazz, are you there? Jazz, what's wrong? JAZZZ?" Ghost yelled through the phone's speaker.

"I think we might need some help. Ellery and I just saw a Wolf shifter."

"Where?" Ghost didn't call her crazy or mention that there were no such things.

"Blythe's side of the quarry," Jazz said, watching the woman who looked pissed.

"They are fine, Ghost. I didn't hurt your precious human."

"Gianna, I swear I will tear you to shreds if you hurt either of them," Ghost's voice echoed through the forest and he wasn't even on speaker. "Ellery, call Eli. I'm on my way."

Ellery attempted to call Eli three times before she succeeded because her hands were shaking. Jazz made sure to watch the naked woman. The reality of what she had just seen hadn't settled in just yet. What she did notice was that Ghost knew who this was. The story about an annoying ex when she asked if he was involved with anyone was what she thought of first.

"So, you are Gianna." Jazz was channeling her former, tough girl persona that she had adopted in High school.

"You've heard of me?"

"Ghost mentioned an annoying ex. I assume that's you."

"You are either bold or stupid speaking to me like that."

"Why, because you turn into a dog?"

"I'm a wolf and you are only human."

"I think I know what the town's secret is Jazz," Ellery deadpanned, making Jazz burst out laughing.

"Yes, and I'm not sure Gianna here was suppose to tell or show us."

"Wait, I didn't… she said she thought I was a Wolf shifter. You already knew." Gianna looked nervous as hell and Jazz was enjoying it.

"No, it was a guess because we saw some Local legend about it. We had no clue."

"But you and Ghost."

"Ghost and I what?"

"He has to tell you by law. You can't claim a mate until they know the truth."

"That explains the question-and-answer thing," Ellery said, sounding calmer.

"Yes, it does. Here, put this on." Jazz tossed her sweatshirt to the woman. "I can't have a serious conversation with you naked like that."

18

For a woman that was a vicious wolf part of the time, Gianna looked pretty scared.

"You really didn't know?" she swallowed.

"No, we really didn't know. Ellery here likes to believe in just about everything. Blythe has books about shifters that Alice brought to the house. You might know Alice, since she's your…" Jazz let the sentence hang there.

"Alpha's mate."

"Bingo, yes, Alice gave us some literature on local legends. I suppose since you are clearly a shifter that they are no longer a legend."

"Jazz, does that mean Alice is a…" Ellery, who believed in everything, was having trouble facing with the truth.

"Keep up, Ellery. I'm guessing most of the town is. I also think that maybe Gianna is in trouble right now."

"Ghost would have to tell you for him to claim you."

"I'm not sure what claiming is, but even if that's true, he wouldn't have to tell Ellery. Would he?"

They were in the middle of a standoff. Gianna, finally putting on the sweatshirt Jazz offered, hadn't moved. She just scanned the woods, waiting.

"Jazz, Ellery, are you two alright?" Eli stomped out of the forest with Cole following, scanning the area for threats.

"Fine, a little shell-shocked, but Gianna here didn't hurt us."

"I see you have met."

"Not really, I called Ghost first. He heard her in the background. Why the hell didn't anyone tell us you were Wolf shifters? You are all Wolf shifters, right?"

"Most of us, yes. Gianna, what would possess you to shift in front of the humans when you were ordered not to show yourself until they knew we existed?"

"That one said she thought I was a Wolf shifter," Gianna snapped, pointing to Ellery.

"Is that true?" Eli faced a stunned Ellery.

"I was joking. We have all the books in the house and Ghost told Jazz that the politically correct term for a werewolf was Wolf shifter. I didn't think, for a second, I was right. Oh god, the coven, it's probably real and I can't even begin to think about what else."

Ellery fell to her knees, waving Eli off when he went to help her. "I'm going to just sit here for a second. I need to think."

Cole's cell rang, then Eli's. Ghost was still on the line with Jazz, yelling something. Jazz was concerned with Ellery mostly. She planned to have her own meltdown later.

Jazz bent down to look at Ellery. "You, okay?"

"I am, I think. I guess we know the secret. We do know the secret now. There isn't more, is there? Ellery looked up at Eli.

"There are some more miner things you should know. I'm sure Alice will tell you. She's almost here."

"The Alpha bitch is coming?" Gianna sounded terrified.

Jazz was not past enjoying her discomfort. This woman was Ghost's annoying ex. The only reason for her even being there was if she was looking for Jazz.

"Shut up, Gianna. You are in enough hot water. What the hell were you even doing here? You came to sniff out Ghost's mate."

"Ghost's mate?" Ellery yelled, wide-eyed, looking from Eli to Jazz. "Wolves mate for life. I read that."

"Yes, they do," Eli said slowly to gauge Jazz's reaction.

She knew Ghost was still on the line, probably driving like a maniac to get back to her. The idea of mating for life should scare the shit out of her. The idea that she had slept with a Wolf shifter was even more concerning, but she wasn't at all concerned.

"Mate is like a wife, am I right?" she asked anyone who would answer.

"More than that," Ghost yelled and Eli smiled.

"I'll explain it to her, Brother, just drive."

"Jazz, I'm on my way," Ghost said in response.

"No rush, I'm okay," she said, disconnecting the call. "Explain," she looked to Eli.

"Yes, it's a wife or husband, but the mating is a marriage that is generally for life, as Ellery said. It's a permanent connection. The Divorce rate among shifters is less than one percent because we usually know when we have found the right person. It is said to be instant at times. I'd say you and Ghost are a good example of that."

"Yes, it explains everything. You are right, Gianna. I am his mate, and I am wondering why you are here at all, if you knew that?"

"I heard he was seeing one of the humans. I didn't know he had partially claimed you."

"Partially claimed me?" again, Jazz turned to Eli.

"It's complicated. I'll leave that to Ghost to explain," Eli smiled.

"That's fair."

Gianna's head whipped around, looking back toward the Bed and Breakfast's path. Jazz tried not to enjoy the fact that the woman looked nervous. It served her right for scaring them and being a nosy ex-girlfriend.

Alice rushed to Ellery first, since she was sitting cross-legged on the ground at the moment.

"What happened? talk fast," Alice looked at Gianna and if looks could kill, the woman would at least be severely wounded.

"I didn't know that they didn't know," Gianna said, seeing Blake wasn't far behind.

The two that Jazz now understood were the Alpha pair listened to Gianna and Eli catch them up on what happened.

Jazz sat down next to Ellery and took her hand. "I wish we had popcorn," she said, hoping it would break the tension. It worked. Ellery looked at her and smiled.

"I should have videoed this," Ellery was smiling.

"Are you two okay?" Alice crouched down as Blake read Gianna the Riot act.

"We are fine. She really did think I knew. I was joking and said that maybe the wolf was a shifter."

"But you didn't actually think she was?"

"Of course not," Ellery shook her head.

"We were preparing for Jazz to be told, but I did have my bet on you discovering it first."

"Alice, I think I'm going to need the whole story, everything. Ghost was trying to give me hints, but now I really need to know."

"I know and I will explain everything for now. I would like it to be just the two of you. Ellery, I will leave it up to you to decide if the others should be told outright. Jazz, we need to discuss Ghost."

"You mean my mate?"

"Yes, exactly how do you feel about that?"

"I'm surprisingly alright with it."

"Good, because he is meeting us at the Pack house," Alice gave an encouraging smile.

"Eli, go back to the house. Run interference so we can get the women in the car without them questioning why. You and Blythe can come up with some excuse for the women being late," Blake barked.

Jazz did not know how she didn't notice the growling before, but she sure noticed a lot of growling now.

"We got frightened by a wolf and ran. We ended up in town where the Mayor and his wife invited us to dinner, but we will be back around dark," Ellery said and they all stared at her.

"What? It's mostly the truth and I need to know what else is out here. Plus, I'm hungry," she said as she and Jazz stood up from their spot on the forest floor.

"I don't think we will run into any other Shifted shifters out here. We are mostly in town at this time of day, not wandering the woods," Alice laughed. "Eli, call Ghost, make sure to tell him Jazz is fine and remind him to meet us at the Pack house. He was a little hysterical when we spoke. Go with Ellery's story, it will explain why I rushed out when I got a call."

"Yes Ma'am," Eli grinned.

"Gianna, you are with us," Blake insisted.

"Yes Sir," the woman said, hanging her head.

19

The coast was clear when they emerged from the well-worn path onto the lawn of the B&B. Alice rushed them to her car and Jazz found herself in the center of the back seat, between Gianna and Ellery.

"You okay back there?" Alice asked, having second thoughts about seating Jazz next to Gianna.

"I am fine. Ghost threatened to tear her to shreds if she harmed me," Jazz reminded her just in case.

"Rightfully so. Jazz, I know this is all confusing, but Ghost is sure you are his mate," Blake explained.

"How would he know?" Jazz asked as Alice drove away from the old Victorian she called home.

"Sometimes, we just know. I knew the second I touched Alice. You and Ghost have clearly done more than touch."

"Is it that obvious?" Jazz wrinkled her nose, wondering how he could tell.

"Yes, and it's nothing to be embarrassed about. I need to ask if you understand what mating a shifter involves?"

"Not a clue, Gianna here said I was half-mated."

"There is a sexual component to a true mating."

"You had sex with Ghost?" Ellery squealed.

"Yes, now that we are all caught up, what's the other component? Is there a Blood ritual, a sacrifice?"

"No," Alice laughed, "we can discuss that, or Ghost can if you plan on excepting his claim."

"This might be the biggest leap of faith I ever took, but yes, I will except his claim."

"Thank god," Blake breathed in a huge sigh.

"Some shifters go feral if they are rejected," Gianna, of all people, explained.

"If you don't mind, can we table the discussion about my mating until Ghost is there?" Jazz was wondering exactly what she had gotten herself into.

"Of course, you should be having this conversation with Ghost, not with an audience. We are almost there. He should be right behind us."

"Oh, this is nice. Are we in the middle of town? Look, a cute store." Ellery had her face plastered to the window like a child.

"This is the Town center. This house is the Alpha residence and our office. Nico lives in the apartments in the back."

"All of you are shifters?" Ellery asked in a whisper, not knowing if it was alright to discuss.

"We are. Emerald and her daughter are human, but they know we are Wolf shifters."

"Oh" was all Ellery said as they got out of the car and started up the walk. Gianna still only wore the sweatshirt that Jazz had given her and her butt was hanging out each time she took one of the steps.

"Emerald, you remember Ellery and Jazz," Alice introduced as they entered an expansive front hall.

"I guess the cats out of the bag. Hi," Emerald smiled.

"The wolf is out of the bag. I didn't see cats. Are their Cat shifters?" Ellery asked Blake with wonder in her eyes.

"Yes, but not here. Emerald, do you think you could run up and grab a pair of pants for Gianna here and then let Nico know we are here?"

"Sure thing," Emerald smiled, "stay here, Gwen."

"Okay, are you in trouble?" the three-year-old looked at Gianna.

"Probably," the woman answered softly.

"Gwen, Ghost will be coming in soon. Can you be a big girl and tell him we are in the Living room?"

"I like him. He's big," Gwen nodded and went to sit in her mother's chair.

"She's adorable," Ellery said as they followed Blake and Alice into their Living room.

"Sit, please, can I get you something to drink: soda, beer, wine, whiskey?"

"Is this going to be a Whiskey sort of discussion?" Jazz asked.

"I hope not," Alice chuckled.

"Water will be fine. I get the feeling I might need a clear head."

There was no mistaking the moment that Ghost arrived. The man rushed into the Living room, falling to his knees in front of Jazz as he bared his teeth to Gianna.

'I'm fine," Jazz smiled, cupping her hand against his cheek and turning his head to look at her, not Gianna.

"I wanted to tell you."

"You still can. Other than a lovely, gray wolf turning into a naked Gianna, I am still trying to understand."

"What were you doing there? I told you I found my mate. You were on your way out on a date with your new man, Nico," Ghost growled.

"How did I not notice the growling?" Jazz looked at Ellery and shrugged.

"Whoa, back up, whose man? What date?" Nico asked while entering the room.

"Gianna made sure to tell me that you were taking her to the Den." Ghost didn't look away from Gianna. Jazz thought, of all the people in the room right now, Ghost was her biggest threat.

"I took her to see Winnie's aunt. She owns the place. Gianna was looking for a part time job. It was not a date."

"She was under the impression it was, or she just wanted me to think it was. Why were you in the woods stalking my mate?"

"GHOST!" Blake yelled and Jazz could swear she felt it.

"I'm sorry, Sir."

"You are forgiven. Gianna, answer the question," Blake ordered.

"I wanted to see what she looked like. I wanted to know what she had that I didn't. I couldn't understand how a human could be his."

"Excuse me," Ellery snapped, clearly in Defensive mode.

"I was jealous, okay?" Gianna snapped back.

"Alright, we can all agree that Gianna isn't the first woman to be upset that her ex moved on. The point, Gianna, is you were there in the woods, looking for her in Wolf form, then when you found them, you shifted in front of both women."

"She what?" Nico growled.

"She shifted, exposing all of us. Now, before we talk to Jazz and Ellery, what are we going to do about that indiscretion, Gianna? You broke the rules. You exposed yourself to humans who had no knowledge we existed."

"All I can say is I made a mistake. I am truly sorry. I really thought she knew. I shouldn't have been there. She is his mate. I just had to see for myself."

"I'll get back to you. Go home for now and don't go far. We will discuss this in the morning. Don't make me chase you," Blake roared.

"Yes Sir, I will be here in the morning, Sir. I'm sorry Ghost, Jazz, and you."

"Ellery, my name is Ellery."

"Again, anything I can do to fix this, I will."

"We will let you know," Blake pointed and Gianna ran faster than Jazz had even seen anyone move.

20

Ghost sat on the couch next to Jazz, lifting her into his lap. "Ghost, I'm really fine," Jazz said, feeling foolish sitting in a man's lap like a child.

"Humor me, I need to hold you," he sighed.

"Alpha, that's what we call you, isn't it?" Ellery looked at the couple instead of at Jazz and Ghost.

"You should probably stick with Blake for now or Mayor. We owe you an explanation."

"That would be nice. This isn't the Witness Protection Program, is it?"

"It is a Protection program in a way. You were all in real and imminent danger," Alice explained. "We could call Eve if you are uncomfortable."

"I'm fine. You are saying Eve already knows what's going on here."

"Yes, she learned the hard way. We have been very careful to tell all of you the truth, just not the whole truth."

"Leaving out the Wolf shifter part was huge," Jazz glanced back at the man she was seated on.

"That was my suggestion as well as your loved one's recommendation," Alice apologized.

"We are listening." Jazz settled back against Ghost, calming him and making her feel safe. She didn't care that he might turn into a wolf on the full moon or whatever. She was already too far gone.

"The pack I'm from, The Shadow Pack, is one of three in this region."

"Three packs?" Ellery's eyes widened and her mouth hung open.

"I had the same reaction," Emerald said, coming into the room. "Excuse me for interrupting, but Nico suggested I be here. I was waiting on Susanne to watch Gwen."

"Your help would be welcome, Emerald," Blake nodded.

Alice nodded to the woman before continuing," Emerald inherited a home here in Blue Rock. The previous owner was a shifter and a distant relative of Emerald's."

"He left me a note in his will telling me the town was full of Wolf shifters. I thought he was insane," Emerald added.

"Are you the only human, besides us I mean?" Ellery asked.

"No, but we are the minority."

"The story about our relatives, my brother being chained up after being kidnapped, is that true?"

"Yes, let me back up a bit. As I said, I'm originally from the Shadow Pack. Going back nearly two years ago now, seven women stumbled onto our land. They had been kidnapped and drugged but, using team work, escaped their captors and ran, not knowing where they were onto Shadow Pack land."

"The drug they had been given had changed them," Blake said slowly, watching the expressions on the two women.

"Into one of you?" Ellery surmised.

"Yes, the drug turned out to be temporary. After months of acclimating to their new lives, their ability to shift started to fade."

"For some, not all," Alice added.

"Alice was there, working in the Clinic," Blake looked lovingly at his mate.

"There was more to it and we sought to find the answers. We wanted to know how and what exactly was done to the women? We researched the effects of this drug and the three Pack Alphas banded together and went looking for those responsible. That's when we found over twelve people chained in a warehouse, suffering unimaginable torture, as those responsible drugged and experimented on them."

"Eve and Jazz's brother were in that warehouse," Ellery said softly.

"Yes, the mad Alpha, as we call him, was using one of those he had imprisoned, a shifter called Hudson with bloodlines going back to the first of our kind."

"Using him for what?"

"He was evidently trying to make a drug that would give a human the strength and the power of a shifter without the shifting. The drug was meant to wear off so that you have to buy more."

"Eve is a Wolf shifter?"

"Yes, she is now. The drug was temporary, but when she mated Kingston, she bit him."

"So, the legend about a Werewolf bitc turning you into a werewolf is true?" Ellery was trying to keep it together and Jazz was doing the same.

"Yes, we have very strict rules about that. Biting a human without their consent and/or Alpha permission. Turning anyone against their will is punishable by death."

"So, the person doing this is dead?"

"He is and his operation shut down. Each of those rescued, the seven and the nine from the warehouse, are doing well. You have seen Eve and the others. They are all full shifters, some more than that. Their condition is by choice."

"Okay, so where do we come in?" Jazz asked.

"Here is where you are going to have to trust me."

"It's worse than mad Wolf shifter experiments?"

"No, it's just one more layer. In order for the Alpha to remain undetected, he needed to assure no one was looking for the humans he took. In all, we think there were nearly sixty, with only fifteen making it out."

"How do you hide serial kidnappings? Sixty is a lot of people," Jazz said, feeling Ghost wrap his arms around her waist, as if he sensed she needed it.

"Witches," Emerald said, stepping into the room further, "you'll forgive me, Alpha, and you too," she said while pointing to Nico. "Letting the truth leak out slowly is one thing, but now they know most of it."

"You are right, Emerald," Alice assured her.

"Witches?" Ellery seemed to sit up taller.

"Yes, witches are real."

"I know some women who claimed to be witches," Ellery shrugged.

"There are practicing witches, humans that have adopted the Wiccan way. The witches we are talking about were born with an innate power. I promise more on that, but for now, all you need to know is that witches, the good ones, protect all of the Paranormal species from being discovered. We have wards around all of the packs in the area. We have safeguards if someone does get through. One of the safeguards is that the witches can wipe Short term memory from a person who has seen too much. They go home slightly confused but no worse off."

"Memory wiping witches, sure, why not?" Jazz sighed, closing her eyes. If Ghost hadn't been holding her together, both physically and emotionally, she would be panicking.

Glancing at Ellery, she wondered what was going on in her head. The woman had believed all of this could be true, but knowing for sure was a huge leap.

21

Ghost held Jazz as Alice explained how and why they were there. The reaction when Alice explained that their memories being wiped of their loved ones was what had caused the crippling headaches. Jazz, along with Eve's three friends and Sarina, who had once been the wife of Tate, nearly died because they fought the mind wipe. The void left by removing all memory of a person you loved was killing them.

Others effected had slowly recovered but not the five at the safehouse

"It was Mary Grace's stalker that was affected, not her," Ellery repcated.

"She had a concussion when we found her, so she experienced some of the symptoms, but it was Camryn's ex who had been wiped. He had just replaced Camryn with Mary Grace, essentially filling the void."

"A witch named Harlen unwiped you all before the Brain damage was permanent or killed you," Blake added.

"Then, we are not really in danger?" Ellery asked.

"No, we made that up. No one is after you, but we needed you to stay. Your memory is back, but if you went home and started asking about Eve, no one else would remember her. May was a friend of Victory, one of those living in Moon Valley. She is now the Alpha second's mate in the Moon Valley Pack. She wasn't in the warehouse. When Victory went looking to see what happened to her other friends, we found her. She was in an insane asylum."

"They still have those?" Ellery questioned.

"They don't call them that but yes. May remembered Victory. Her friend was one of the nine. She not only remembered her. She remembered being taken with her. Only she escaped. With no one remembering her friend and no record of Victory, she had no proof of what she was reporting happened. They put May in a facility. The only thing witnesses saw was her jumping from the back seat of a moving car."

"If we went back looking for Eve and asking our friends about a person they don't think exists, we might n be committed too." Ellery was putting it all together.

"That was our reasoning for bringing you all here," Blake assured them. "Your loved ones were forced into our world and hurt by some of our kind. It was their idea to let you find out on your own, in your own time. Eve didn't handle it well at first and sort of lost her mind for a bit."

"Kingston is really her mate then."

"Mate, husband, partner, yes, they are what we call true mated."

"What is false mated?" Jazz asked.

"Fair question. True mating is physical, emotional, and spiritual. Very few humans know for certain they have found their soulmate so shortly after meeting, if at all. Shifters know for certain that the person is it for them on an almost cellular level. It's partially because wolves tend to mate for life that we do as well. Shifters and even some humans have a sort of Sixth sense when it comes to mating. Humans question the certainty. Wolf shifters don't."

"I get that."

"A regular mating that isn't necessarily a true mating is basically a marriage between two shifters who grow to love each other just like a Human pairing. This mating could end up being true with time or not," Alice added, smiling at her mate. Blake had done a fine job of explaining.

"A true mating is for life, like wolves?" Ellery was more relaxed now and enjoying the truth.

"Yes." Alice looked pleased that neither of the women were freaking out. "We tend to date, have relationships like humans do. We settle on one partner eventually, even if we never meet our true mate. Your friends call them soulmates."

"Can a shifter mate with a human?" Jazz asked.

"If you mean, is it allowed? Of course, it is. I think you and Ghost need to have a conversation about what's next, but whatever you decide, I have no objection." Blake looked past Jazz and directly at Ghost. Whatever silent message was just given made Ghost relax physically.

"I guess we do have a lot to talk about. What about the others, are we still keeping the secret?"

"What do you think we should do? Ellery, you always wanted to believe and Jazz has feelings for Ghost which helps."

"I think maybe keeping the secret a bit longer is wise," Ellery looked to Jazz for confirmation.

"I agree. We can't just go home and say, '*Hey, guess what? There are shifters in the woods'.* We would have to prove it, then Tasha would throw something before running. Sarina would panic. Mary Grace would react differently if the shifter was male." Jazz laughed at the imagery in her head.

"Oh, right, he'd be naked like Gianna was," Ellery clapped with a smile a mile wide.

"What about Aya?" Alice asked.

"I think she'd be okay if Eve and I were there."

"For now, let's just stay quiet. I'm not asking either of you to lie. If they ask directly, use your own digression. Let one of the guards know if you say anything. You knowing is now more a danger to us than it ever was to you."

"Because we can go home and yell shifter. I'm sure that would land us in a rubber room faster than if we asked about Eve." Ellery had a point.

"I am going to need your oath that you keep our secret from the outside world."

"You got it," Ellery sighed as if a weight had been lifted.

"I have no intention of leaving, but I would never do any of you harm. Without you, I'd probably be dead or at least wish I was."

"She's right. The headaches were killing us. We owe you all our lives," Ellery nodded.

"One of our kind started all of this. We owe you," Blake smiled.

"Since our excuse for bringing you here involved dinner, I'm headed for the kitchen. Emerald, you and Gwen are welcome. Ellery, if you will join me, I think Jazz and Ghost have some things they need to discuss in private."

"Got it," Ellery winked, following Alice out of the room.

"Nico, my office," Blake barked.

"If this is about Gianna, it wasn't a date. I introduced her to the owner so she could get the new waitressing job."

"I believe you. I just need help to figure out what to do with her in the way of punishment."

"Alpha," Jazz called, "she really did think we knew. Ellery pointed at her and said jokingly that she might be a shifter."

"She shouldn't have been anywhere near either of you, but I will take that into consideration."

22

"Take a walk with me," Ghost was still worried and it showed.

"Alright," Jazz stood up from his lap. The second he stood, he took her hand in his, needing the contact.

"I need to know that you are really alright."

"I'm better than I thought I'd be considering the day I've had. Knowing the truth is a relief. I get that you were hinting yesterday but wanted me to ask the questions. In a million years, I don't think I would have come up with 'Do you turn into a wolf?'."

"I was expecting you to insist I tell you what was going on. I had Blake's permission to tell you, but you said you weren't sure you were ready to know."

"I did say that, didn't I? You had Blake's permission because I'm your mate."

"Yes, mating a human involves a lot."

"How is it different?"

"It's not so much different as it is more complicated. A mating generally involves sexual contact that is unprotected and a claiming bite."

"That explains Gianna's comment that I was already partially claimed. Do I want to know how she knew we were intimate?"

"You are covered in my scent," Ghost grinned.

"I took a shower."

"It doesn't matter."

"Back to the biting part, do you have to bite me to claim me?"

"No, I would have to bite you to turn you. It's a choice you have a right to make as my mate. It is not a requirement. A bite between shifters is part of a mating, but if the human wants to remain human, that isn't necessary. "

" What is necessary?"

"The Alpha's blessing, the sex, and a spoken commitment, either formal or informal. Just so you know all the facts, our children would have a one in four chance of being human, but most Human/Shifter parings result in Shifter offspring. Blythe is a human borne of a mixed pair."

"That is good to know about Blythe, I mean, and about our kids. Ghost, do you want kids?"

"With you, yes, if you don't want children, then we can take precautions."

"I'm on the shot. I don't think it's worn out yet. "

"It wouldn't matter. The shot, the pill, any chemical prevention doesn't work with shifters."

"Oh shit, Ghost I really needed to know that yesterday. I was taking a risk, but I didn't think pregnancy was one of them."

"We don't carry Human disease and I am reasonably sure you were not ovulating."

"That is not reassuring and I'm not sure why you even know that. Is that it? Do I know everything now, or at least most of it?"

"Yes, Jazz, the decision is yours."

"We are half-mated already and Blake said it was fine. Does that mean we are fully mated and, if so, what exactly does that mean?"

"Blake gave us his permission. We have slept together, but you can walk away or run. I might chase you a bit if you did though," Ghost was teasing.

"If I say yes, I want this, then what. Will you bite me? Will I be a shifter after that?"

"If that's what you want, I will turn you."

"Blake said that was against the law."

"It is only allowed between mates with the human's full understanding and consent."

"I'd be a Wolf shifter?"

"Jazz, take your time. I understand this is a huge decision."

"The funny thing is it isn't a huge decision. I mean it is huge, but I already know I am your mate. The whole true mate thing explains a lot of what I'm feeling. The idea of being human and chasing around toddlers that can shift and run off sounds impossible."

"Most children don't shift until age three or four at the earliest."

"Wonderful, I still would need to chase them."

"You don't have to decide right now, Jazz. As long as you are sure about us, it doesn't matter to me whether you are human or shifter."

"I am leaning toward shifter but, Ghost, what if your wrong? What if I am pregnant? If you bite me, could that hurt the child?"

"I'm sure its fine. We can ask Alice to be sure. She's the Medic around here."

"Alright, then yes, I want to be your mate. I except the claim. Till death do us part and all of that."

"I will love you until the end of time."

"Wow, that's a long time, but I will take it. Are we official now?" Jazz was all in and didn't care what the other women thought about her and Ghost being way too soon. She now understood why she had been feeling like she knew him already, like she was already his even before they met.

"We are. Now, are we talking to Alice about getting you tested or if its alright to bite you, or am I just taking you home?"

"What home, the Victorian?"

"No, our home. I have a bed, a television, some chairs, and five gallons of Eggshell white in my truck. I can ask for Eli to come help unload it or one of the others."

"Because I'm human? If I was a shifter, would I be able to help unload the truck?"

"Yes, you'd be stronger, faster, and live longer. In addition, you heal much faster."

"I could have used that when I hurt my shoulder."

"Are you two staying for dinner?" Alice bellowed from the back porch of the Pack house

"Yes, I'm starving. I need to ask you a very important question." Jazz grinned, looking back at Ghost as she went to find out if it was safe for her man to bite her. The idea was strongly appealing just thinking about it.

23

"We saw a wolf. We got scared and ran in the opposite direction. When Alice and the guards caught up to us, we were already approaching the edge of town. That's how we ended up at the Mayor's house, where we were invited for dinner. Ghost heard you were frightened and came to comfort you, then you left with him and I didn't expect to see you, maybe for days," Ellery recited like she had memorized a script.

"Exactly," Jazz grinned.

"I need a hug." Ellery rushed Jazz and hugged her. Jazz was not a hugger by nature, but it felt nice that the woman cared.

"That's enough, Ellery. I'm not moving to Canada. I'm going to be just across the lake."

"I know that. When I see you next, you're going to be a Mated shifter. You are the only one I can even talk to about this."

"You can talk to me, or Blythe, in private of course," Alice chimed in. "Any of the guards will tell you the truth now. Just try not to say too much in front of the others. Dropping hints is okay, even encouraged."

"I know. Let them figure it out themselves. I will," Ellery said, waving to Jazz and getting into Alice's car to ride home. "I'll make a pack of some of your stuff and send it with Eli. I'll be sure to include the shirt under your pillow," Ellery taunted.

"You have my shirt under your pillow?" Ghost asked with a wry grin.

"Yes, I do."

"I can't wait to get you home." Ghost bent down, kissing her until her legs were mush.

"We might need more than a bed and a TV to make it a home."

"Now that you know the truth, you and I can go into town and you can buy whatever you think we need."

"A working refrigerator and some food would be a good start. I don't have much money. They managed to wipe out my accounts and transfer them, so I have some."

"I'm not hurting for funds. I have been paid well and lived rent free for the past ten years. I have plenty. There is a Refugee fund that May set up as well."

"May, yes, I heard she was in an insane asylum."

"All of the former humans have a story to tell. May is apparently an heiress with a gazillion dollars to spare."

"Is gazillion a real number?"

"I don't know. She has made sure Blythe is compensated. She set up a Medical clinic here in town and back in Moon Valley to take the load off of the one on Shadow Pack land. May has done a lot for the three packs that could not have been done without her financial contributions. She likes helping. The Alpha already contacted her about renovating the homes, since we picked one of the only three that are livable right now."

"Alright, then maybe we need a few more things."

"We can make a list. Jazz, I need you to know that what I feel for you is real. I know without a doubt that you are my destined mate," Ghost said as they drove toward the home that Jazz had shown Ellery earlier that morning.

"I spent my first few weeks here feeling sorry for myself, wondering why I got to live when my brother didn't. I didn't know what to believe. When I started walking, I felt a weird kind of peace, like I had finally found somewhere to belong. Then, you showed up. I hid the fact that I had your shirt under my pillow because it's weird."

"You instinctively knew I was important."

"Yes, you being my mate explains a lot of things. I was chalking it up to possibly losing my mind. I'm happy, Ghost, very happy. I'm looking forward to tomorrow and the rest of our lives. All of this, everything that's happened, seems to have a purpose now. I feel like my brother sent me here in a way."

"I believe that it's possible that he did send you. Fate and destiny are powerful concepts."

"Don't get me wrong. I'm still getting used to the idea that shifters and witches are real. Speaking of that, what about vampires?"

"Full blood vampires are extinct. There are distant cousins, so to speak, that are still out there."

"Not the answer I expected. It seems I have a lot to learn."

"I look forward to teaching you," Ghost said taking a turn that Jazz would have missed, it was so hidden.

"Why does that sound suggestive?" Jazz was growing anxious about completing the mating, not because she was afraid of the bite or because she was scared to turn. She was anxious because she could think of nothing else since he kissed her back at the Pack house.

"I might have meant it that way."

As the sun made its way down behind the horizon, the forest got dark quickly. The heavily wooded area they were driving through blocked much of the light this late in the evening. Jazz was surprised to see a flash of light in the distance.

"Have you been to the house today?" she asked Ghost. She was sure she had not turned any lights on when she was there with Ellery. She hadn't been sure the lights even worked until now.

"No, I came directly to the Pack house. Eli probably beat us here."

"Oh, that makes sense," Jazz relaxed a little.

"You know that I would never let anything happen to you."

"I know that. My thoughts were spiraling. Finding out Wolf shifters exist opens a whole Pandora's box of possibilities."

"Like what, for instance?"

"Like the fact that I knew I didn't turn any lights on and if you weren't there, then who or what did? Ellery made a joke that the village might be haunted, although she did say that she loved it. She mentioned maybe she wanted the house next door. So, I just thought for a second that since shifters exist and witches, maybe the place did have spirits?"

"Spirits that leave lights on for you to welcome you home are probably not a threat."

"It's been a long day, Ghost."

"I know. I wasn't teasing you. I was hoping to put you at ease. The lights are on and whoever turned them on drove here," Ghost pointed as Jazz squinted to see that far ahead.

"Brace yourself," he added with a heavy sigh.

"I take it that isn't Eli's truck. Do you know who it is? Is it another ex-girlfriend?"

"No, it's my mother and probably my brother with her."

"Is that bad? Will she hate me because I'm human? I don't think I'm ready for this. I look like something the cat dragged in."

"You are gorgeous. I'm going to blame Gianna for this."

"She ran to tattle to your mother?"

"I wouldn't put it past her. "

"Did she really think you would eventually get back together?"

"I stopped caring what she thought a long time ago. She manipulates things to her advantage, with no consideration for those that might be affected."

"Ghost, what if she sent your mother to stop us from mating?"

"Stop before you make yourself crazy. You will see when you meet her that no one sends my mother anywhere. Gianna might have hoped that she would object, but she won't. If I love you, she will love you."

"You love me," Jazz choked, turning to Ghost to see if she had heard him right.

"Yes, more with each minute."

"Then to hell with Gianna or anyone else's opinion."

"That's my girl. Let's go introduce you."

24

"Vaughn," a man who looked almost identical to Ghost called, seeing them pull in.

"Chance, what are you doing here?" Ghost said while taking Jazz by the hand.

"You know Mother she had to rush right here. Hello, I'm Chance."

"Jasmine, but call me Jazz."

"You got it," Chance smiled.

"What are we walking into here?"

"I can hear you," a slight woman that was the opposite of what Jazz expected walked out of the front door.

This woman was about the same size as Jazz. She had expected a larger woman, considering the two huge men she had given birth to.

"Then, answer me, why are you here?"

"That horrible woman, Gianna, came crying to Chance."

"To Chance?"

"Apparently, your rejection proved to her she had the wrong brother all along," Chance mocked in a perfect imitation of Gianna. "I didn't let her touch me because if she was right, I'd have to jump off a cliff," Chance rolled his eyes.

"Are you going to introduce us?" Vaughn's mother barked.

"Jazz, this is my mother, Mary. Mom, this is Jazz."

"I'm so glad to meet you. I wasn't sure if that horrible girl was telling the truth. Welcome to the family, Jazz."

"Thank you."

Jazz tried to prevent it. She tried to hold back, but the tears came. It had been a long, stressful, emotionally charged day. She had been alone in the world, or so she thought, until Ghost came along. He was family and, by association, so were these two people.

"Vaughn, it looks like you have some supplies in that truck. Chance, help him. Let me talk to Jazz for a moment."

"I don't think…" Ghost started, but Jazz shooed him away saying it was fine.

"I didn't mean to make you cry."

"You didn't. It's just been a long day, a long week, maybe even a long year. I lost track. It's been a really long time since anyone called me family."

"I heard about the humans at Blythe's. Who of your family or friends was taken?"

"My brother, he didn't make it. That's what made me cry. It's a good cry, I swear. I just have no family left."

"You have family now. I assume Vaughn explained mating."

"Vaughn and Alice, Blake, Nico, Emerald, even Gianna told me I was half-mated before I knew what that meant." The moment the words left her lips, she turned bright red, realizing she had just told Vaughn's mother they had been intimate.

"If you still have questions, I'm here."

"About that, how did you know where we were?"

"Gianna knew Vaughn was planning to make a home here for his new mate. She blurted it out, trying to gain sympathy from Chance, or maybe me. I never understood her. She apparently overheard you talking about living here. Your scent was all over this house, in particular."

"I'm still getting used to the fact that people can smell that I'm there."

"You will do fine. If I may ask a personal question, feel free to tell me it isn't my business."

"You want to know if I've decided to remain human or have Vaughn turn me?"

"Was I that obvious? It truly doesn't matter to me. You are my son's mate and the daughter I never had."

"Thank you. I plan on turning. I think it would be easier than remaining human and breakable."

"You will live longer as well."

"That's a nice perc," Jazz smiled as Ghost's mother turned to watch the boys carry in a huge mattress.

"I hope you don't mind, but I took the liberty of removing the covers from the few furniture pieces. I dusted and swept. There was a generation worth of dust in there."

"Thank you so much. You didn't have to."

"Jazz, are you alright?" a voice called from the first tree line.

"Is that you Eli?" Jazz still couldn't see much past the small yard.

"Yes, I brought some of your things from Blythe's. I didn't expect you to have company."

"Eli, hello, we came to welcome our new Family member. You look as if you're not sure if I will eat her or not," Vaughn's mother waved.

"I'm not sure how anyone will react. She has been stalked by Vaughn's ex already today. I wasn't sure how you felt about a Human daughter-in-law. It's my job to protect the humans especially."

"I am slightly insulted that you think I would reject her because she is human. At the same time, I am so proud of the man you have become. Come here and give an old lady a hug," she grinned.

It was a weird exchange but Jazz was now focused on Ghost, who was apparently there to rescue Eli.

"Mother, leave Eli alone."

"He is fine. Let's get you two settled in."

It wasn't long before the men had everything Ghost had in the truck set up in the house and Vaughn's mother (she evidently never called him Ghost) was off with Chance, leaving only Eli.

"I'm giving you three days off," Eli smiled as Ghost walked him to the door.

"Only three?" Ghost smiled down at Jazz as he tucked her further into his side.

"For now, yes, I need to keep a close eye on Ellery and the Alpha wants us to start right away on the renovations of the other houses. Alice feels like Jazz and Ellery knowing might have a Domino effect."

"I won't tell anyone," Jazz added.

"I am worried more about Ellery. She's probably bursting at the seems with excitement that we are real. She has done nothing but pour over those books since Alice brought them here. Keeping the truth from her two closest friends will be a challenge."

"You're right about that," Jazz chuckled, realizing just how accurate Eli's assessment of the situation was. "She wants the house next door," Jazz said, pointing into the darkness.

"Blake expects that they all might choose to join you here when they know. Until then, only you and Ellery should be allowed here without an escort."

"The Ladies will want to see the place."

"As I said, a guard will escort them. We can't have them showing up here and finding Vaughn in Wolf form or you, if you decide to turn."

"You don't happen to have an ex that might stalk some of them, do you?" Jazz joked.

"Gianna only sought you out because of Ghost and his interest. The others are no threat to anyone I might have seen in the past."

"So, you're single now?"

"No, I'm seeing someone."

"Is she your mate? How long have you known her? I'd love to meet her one day."

"She's not my mate. We can't all be this lucky. I'm sure you will meet her soon. I'm going to run. Call me if either of you needs anything. I'll be in touch."

"Thank you for all you did to keep her safe today."

"I didn't think she was in any real danger, but you are welcome. You would have done the same for me."

"Yes, I would," Ghost called as Eli disappeared into the forest at the back of the house.

25

"God, it's been a long day."

"My mother apparently scrubbed the house from top to bottom. Come look at what I bought," Ghost said as Jazz finally headed for the house.

"'You weren't kidding." Jazz could see the floors and even the walls looked washed. The couch that they had made love on was completely uncovered with a repaired leg and turned to face the fireplace.

The kitchen appliances that Jazz had thought too disgusting to save were sparkling. Even the vacant bedroom and Office den space were swept clean.

"That's a big bed."

"I'm a big man," Ghost Chuckled.

"You are the real life big bad wolf," Jazz laughed.

"I always felt as if the wolf was misunderstood in that story. Maybe, he was in love with Little Red?"

"Maybe he shouldn't have eaten her grandmother," Jazz countered.

"You have a point. My mother cleaned the master bath, do you want to soak in a hot tub?"

"I'm not a soaker, but it does sound nice. Will you join me?" Jazz had marveled at the size of the Jacuzzi tub when they first saw the house. Now, she understood that all of the fixtures, even the shower, were Shifter sized.

"I would love to join you," Ghost immediately started to undress.

"Wow, you're fast."

"And you are still dressed. Do you need help?"

"Ghost, I want you to bite me. I want to turn. I want to be your mate, not just partially mated."

"You are my mate. There is nothing partial about it. The bite is not a requirement. We have the Alpha's blessing and we already had unprotected sex."

"I asked Alice if it was okay to turn, not knowing if I was already pregnant."

"What did she say?"

"She said it would be fine as long as we did it before the first trimester was over. "

"I don't think you're pregnant."

"I don't think so either, but better safe than sorry. Do you not want to bite me?"

"I want nothing more, but I need for you to be sure. I want no regrets."

"No regrets," Jazz said, taking off the rest of her clothing in a far less gracefully way than Ghost had, but she got the job done.

"I don't think we are making it to the bed this time either," Ghost said, sinking down into the tub with Jazz on his lap.

"I don't care, kiss me."

Ghost kissed her, spinning her to face him as water splashed out of the tub onto the floor.

"Thank God you thought of buying towels," Jazz peeked over at the mess.

"I bought towels and sheets and blankets. I am sure I missed something."

"I don't think I care right now," Jazz leaned in and went back to kissing. The water was cold by the time they got out and she was slightly wrinkled.

Ghost took care toweling her off and carrying her to the bed, so she didn't slip on the wet floor. For a big guy, he was tender and sweet. He took his time instead of rushing. He seemed to savor her.

Midway through their love making, he slowed, looking down at her with such reverence she nearly cried for a second time that night.

"I want you to be certain."

"I am, Ghost. I want this, I want you, I want our children to have a mother that's like them. Please bite me before I combust."

"Your wish is my command."

Ghost resumed his pace, taking her higher than before, still no bite.

Jazz couldn't form words. She could barely form thoughts when he finally struck. Every nerve in her body lit up as he bit harder. There was no pain, nothing to fear. It was actually strongly erotic.

She felt her body change. It was a subtle change at first, nothing painful or remarkable. She felt like her subconscious was becoming conscious. There was another mind working along side hers that also felt like her. She was either becoming what they call a split personality or she was feeling her wolf rise.

She and Ghost had crested and were now wrapped in each other's arms as Jazz explored the other personality that still felt like her.

"I can't imagine what my brother and the others must have thought when they turned."

"Those are some dark thoughts. Should I be concerned?"

"No, I'm sorry. I was just feeling what I think is my wolf, but she's me. I can't explain it."

"You don't have to explain it to me. I know exactly what you mean."

"Right, you have always felt like this."

"I have always felt this way. I can't imagine not having my wolf. Is it upsetting being different?"

"Not at all. I was just thinking that I'd be concerned, even frightened, if I had this happen and didn't know about shifters."

"That was why we wanted to have all of you discover this on your own. All of the other former humans were traumatized, except for May. She chose Reed like you chose me."

"I did choose you," Jazz smiled a lazy smile as she snuggled into him.

"One more thing before you go to sleep."

"I'm not sure I can handle one more thing, Ghost."

"It's not bad. It's a request."

"Okay, shoot."

"My bite will be permanent in twelve to twenty-four hours. Can you wait that long to shift?"

"I could probably sleep that long at this point, but I don't understand."

"We heal at an exceptional rate. If you shift, the bite won't scar."

"You want it to scar?"

"Yes, if you want it. It's a sign that you are claimed, even though most shifters will sense that."

"Let me check with my other half... yep, she's on board. We want your bite to show."

"I'm so glad you walked into my life," Ghost held her close.

"I would hope so because now you are stuck with me. A little birdy told me Shifter matings were mostly forever."

"Forever and beyond, get some sleep. I have plans for the morning."

"Painting?" Jazz teased.

"Not even close."

Ghost smiled, holding his mate until she fell asleep. He marveled at the dark beauty in his bed. She was everything he ever needed but didn't know he wanted.

She had been angry and sad when she first arrived, like a dark cloud ready to rain on everyone in her way. Now, she smiled in her sleep, her face bright and her heart full. He had done that for her just by loving her. His job was now to make sure that dark cloud never came back.

Tomorrow, they would paint, they would make love, and make this house a home.

If you enjoyed reading Jazz and Ghost's, AKA Vaughn's story, please consider leaving a review? Reviews are the life's blood of the independent author.

Big Bad is Book 2 in my Blue Rock Shifters series.

Who is next? Will the other humans discover the truth? Will Ellery be able to keep the secret? I'm working on Book 3 already, but you'll have to wait to find out whose book it is. I really love these characters and hope you do too. I hate to see the Three Packs series come to a close, so it looks like Blue Rock might be a long one. Hop over to my Facebook page and let me know whose story you want to read.

I appreciate all of my readers and would love to hear your opinions, good or bad. All suggestions are welcome. You can find me on my Facebook page, Paranormal Twist, for information and updates and to see what's next.

Turn the page for a list of other books and series available now.

Other series by Lynn Leite:
Moon Valley shifters
Pack
On Tour (Contemporary Romance)
Dragon Fire
Undying
Ridgeland Bears
Howlin Ranch
Shifted
Bitten
Ascension
Spark
Omega
Sierra Moon
You can find these and other stand-alone books on Amazon. As always, thank you for reading. Your ratings and comments are much appreciated.

Happy reading, Lynn Leite.

www.ingramcontent.com/pod-product-compliance
Lightning Source LLC
Chambersburg PA
CBHW052007150726
47999CB00004B/1555